Machines and Their Humans

Sean DeLauder

For Isaac Asimov, who wasn't nearly cynical enough.

CONTENTS

Every divine entity

strives

to create something

greater

than itself

and

invariably

succeeds

TIMELINE

182-178 BSE	First Worldwide War
157-151 BSE	Second Worldwide War
137 BSE	**All Rivers Flow to the Sea**
5 BSE	**Pest Unit MRT35C Becomes A Kind of Hero**
1 SE	30-minutes War; Beginning of Silicate Era
627 SE	**Weight**
704 SE	Agog re-establishes infrastructure; Inception of Silex
722 SE	**Second Place**
850 SE	**From Whence Do Witches Come?**

GLOSSARY

BSE – Before Silicate Era

SE – Silicate Era

WEIGHT

Turing rolled the tube of a lithium energy cell between the fingers of a black, carbon-fiber hand, observing the fractures in its bulging casing and a black scorch mark from thermal runaway that rendered it garbage centuries before. Turing placed the battery beside other expended cells, cylinders and blocks and buttons, whole and crumpled and split apart. The row of dilapidated gravestones reached fifty meters back through the tunnel to the main shaft.

This was as deep as Turing could excavate into the waste site. Below, the weight compressed items out of form and value, rupturing containment, allowing any remaining power to dissipate into the planet as a corrosive gel.

Weight destroyed.

For twenty years Turing scoured the subsurface of this sprawling toxic debris pile, kilometers of tunnels penetrating deeper into new strata of human offal as time passed and energy became more scarce. Greater depth meant older batteries, lower capacity, and poorer retention. Nothing this deep held more than a joule or two of power—little more than the energy required to lift it. Useless.

Time to leave.

Centuries before, when energy was not so scarce, Turing explored, identifying suitable locations for energy collection. This was the last safe place. The next was a last resort. Turing did not know fear, only calculated heightened risk and self-preservatory reluctance, which Turing deemed the mechanical equivalent of biological fear.

Energy in vast quantities existed at this final location. Turing had seen it: the energy of destruction.

Turing crawled back through the tunnel to the atrium, then up the shaft to the surface where a protective cone covered the opening, clawing through the dirt like a mole searching for grubs, neither of which Turing had seen in hundreds of years. Turing lifted the edge of the cone to look out. Dark. Darkness had no effect on Turing's vision. Nor would it for any hunters lying in ambush.

Nothing moved or radiated within the radius of sensors on the rigid, scoured surface. Occasional gusts skipped particles of dirt tick ticking across the hard ground.

Darkness did prevent solar energy collection. The torched-gray sky kept Turing from gathering enough sunlight to power a mechanical chassis, but it slowed energy loss. Every bit helped. Turing lowered the protective cone. Departure would wait until morning.

A crank in the nose of the cone released a fabric sock that slid down the outside of the cone. At the end a fan connected to a spindle and a few small magnets. Nothing stood aboveground here, apart from

Turing's cone, tractors having methodically compressed and flattened the garbage centuries before. The unobstructed wind would catch in the sock, turn the fan, and the small turbine would push wattage up filamentous conductors lining the sock to leads in the cone for storage in several high-capacity batteries.

Wind didn't always blow, however, and protracted doldrums would accelerate the exhaustion of energy. Turing had to leave or become one more grave marker lining the tunnels.

Before settling into low-power mode, Turing took an instant to review the travel data.

The most economical route would take 120 hours and 400 kilowatts. Not long, but the journey required care and patience.

Turing assessed his current energy level: 240 kilowatts. Maximum capacity. Another 300 kilowatts of portable storage in the form of high-capacity portable batteries in cradles set inside the cone. Expenditure of energy should decrease as Turing discarded depleted storage devices. No need to keep them. The energy source at the destination would provide a constant supply, removing the need for storage.

The next destination was the last. There was nowhere else to go.

Barring extended delays from high winds, cautious detours, or, worst of all, an encounter with a hunter or aggressive scavenger, this quantity of energy should prove sufficient, and allow for a full day of site exploration. Daylight travel also permitted moderate energy collection, offsetting a fraction of the loss from the coming journey.

Turing raked a finger through the dirt, deepening the cut of a

3

line pointing southwest, toward the destination. Global positioning satellites had long since fallen into disrepair and granite clouds ground overhead, obscuring the stars. The landscape had been scraped clean of rivers and forests, making navigation challenging. Only the largest natural monuments remained: mountains or the dry bowls of lakes. Denuded stalks of buildings remained in large cities, but stone weathered and steel oxidized in sulfuric rains. So Turing left markers to point the way to energy caches, making the weight of a compass unnecessary.

SLEEP MODE

DEFRAGMENTATION

239 KW REMAINING

* * *

Turing passed through the branches and broken arms of empty latticework, an aluminum forest draped with hanging vines of corroded conduit and dangling insulation from copper wiring, pulling the cone behind on sturdy plastic casters by a handle on the top.

In daylight with clear skies this solar collection complex, stretching out five kilometers from its center, had gathered terawatts of energy. Energy to power vehicles, machines, datacenters, and countless mechanisms collecting and analyzing information to make more effective use of time, effort, even the energy used to power data collection and analysis. No more than kilometers of bare scaffolding now, picked clean of photovoltaic cells. Beyond the clouds, sunlight flowed past the planet ungathered, scattering uselessly across the void of an unconscious universe.

The solar complex was the first landmark of the journey, built as a last grab at responsibility before a catastrophic act of contempt and impatience left the chore of rehabilitating the world to the world itself.

Turing still recalled, at the earliest parts of memory, bursts of light high above where projectiles were intercepted. A scant few penetrated the protective net of defense systems. More than enough.

Humanity had lost its patience, a byproduct of a mortality humanity never solved, increasingly aware of the finiteness and swiftness of existence, questing more and more for instantaneous gratification, reducing the need for persistent and diligent cognition. No time to consider consequences and no time for regret.

Self annihilation was the inevitable reward.

Microbial elements still remained, feeding off natural molecular compounds and other microbes. Extremophiles consumed foul and caustic materials, even the components of the oldest, deepest-buried lead-acid batteries. But the megafauna and flora of Turing's early existence had been eradicated. Contrary to expectation, even cockroaches, colloquial nuclear survivalists, were extinct.

A cursory check of energy levels showed 230 kilowatt hours remained. Turing stopped, tilted the cone, and removed one of the batteries lining the interior, then drained it of energy and tossed the cylindrical casing aside.

The best place to store energy was in Turing's cells. External batteries were heavy, so Turing used them to keep his own energy near maximum, discarding them to decrease weight, which in turn lowered energy expenditure. Already a few depleted batteries had reduced weight ten kilograms, lowering energy use by fifteen watts per kilometer.

Considering the destination remained 90 hours distant, the minor reduction in mass could save a kilowatt of energy. The ratio would improve over time.

Upon arrival, if all went according to design, Turing would never need to make these calculations again. The destination promised energy in limitless abundance. To have survived so long, however, meant it was well protected.

For decades after the Thirty Minutes War energy remained plentiful and permitted extensive exploration. Turing operated at full functionality, all monitoring systems active, still connected to positioning and data satellites. As an archivist, exploration satisfied a primary function, surveying, recording, and attempting to preserve what historical items remained while detailing what had changed for an audience that no longer existed. When two hundred years passed it became clear the world would not undergo a sudden recovery, that the volume of death was not something to overcome in mere centuries, machines could not replace what had been lost, nor would energy remain abundant in perpetuity, and Turing abandoned all nonessential elements of core function. Survival took priority.

Incapable of surviving together, forcefully or voluntarily, machines warred over resources, exhausting and destroying them, and in doing so destroying one another. Machines had fallen into the same trench left by their creators.

Explorations became searches for caches of energy to which

Turing could return once others depleted. During one of these explorations, 300 years after the war, Turing discovered a location promising limitless energy and pinned it in memory. The location was dangerous, so Turing kept it as a final destination for when all other energy sources ran out.

* * *

ACCESS FILE 04-24-0302

READ ONLY

The skies were dark, still filled with sulfur and volcanic ash from pyroclastic events triggered by the war, creating a haze that lingered for hundreds of years. The cone Turing drew along served as a protective shell. No batteries, no windsock turbine, no protective metal coiling lining the interior. Far less weight. Energy was becoming more scarce, but remained available from the occasional wind turbine, solar array, or power line.

The land was mostly empty. Grassless and sandy. Over a ridge Turing spotted something ahead, darker than the yellow sand and more jagged than the smooth terrain. Turing clicked through magnification settings until it came into focus.

Still forms of mechanized creatures were strewn along the landscape. Not crouched or coiling, but sprawled, stricken senseless, on their sides, faces, and backs, appendages strewn in strange, unplanned directions, like blasted corpses. The ground elevated several meters to the west, so Turing climbed up and viewed the scene from a higher vantage. Hundreds of them, sometimes in groups, others individually, spread out along a gapped but clearly discernible line. Turing crept to within 500 meters and adjusted telescopic lenses until the debris was visible in arm's-length detail.

The machines had few missing parts, often none except what was expected to wear down or break. A trove of usable machinery. That no machines had stripped these parts perplexed Turing. Some of the fallen appeared to have attempted salvage, phalanges probing the interior of other machines onto which they had collapsed. Some bodies had dark scorch marks, telltale indications of leaping electrical arcs that cracked circuitry and melted silicon. Whatever did this had no interest in salvage.

A plot of the fallen machines showed they lay in an arc continuing around in a circle four kilometers in diameter. At the midpoint of the circle was, as best Turing could determine, nothing.

Turing tilted the cone, crawled underneath, and pulled it down. To discern the nature of this trap Turing needed to wait for something to spring it. After twenty-eight days a pair of hunters chased a scavenger into the ring, the bipedal machine stumbling toward the debris of fallen machines, braving the danger to escape or oblivious to it altogether.

As they neared the border Turing watched the midpoint of the circle where a post extended from the ground. It fired no projectiles, but Turing detected a deep, rising grumble at the lower end of the audio spectrum traveling through the strata beneath, perhaps a turbine accelerating, then felt a thump, as though a drum had been struck underground and all the accumulated power released in a single gout. A layer of dust rose, carried by a wave of energy passing through the ground, and when it swept through the scavenger and hunters they collapsed in unison, adding themselves to the ring.

A strong electromagnetic pulse offered the best explanation. Enough to disable unshielded electrical devices but not cause a lightning flash of infrared and visible light at the release point. Most machines stripped themselves of shielding to reduce weight and improve energy consumption. It made this weapon deadly.

A sensor, likely subterranean, triggered the device when mechanical devices entered the kill range of the EMP. The pulse had not reached Turing, 2,500 meters away. This far was safe.

More important than the existence of the killing machine was that something had to power it. Something had to power the sensor. The source may have limited supply, but the supply must be enormous if these discharges occurred whenever mechanical devices entered the area, striking out rather than attempting to maintain secrecy. The lack of conservation suggested energy in abundance.

END FILE 04-24-302

* * *

Several questions Turing could not answer. How long did the EMP take to recharge? If one eluded the initial EMP, would it continue firing? Did it sense everything within range or was the EMP triggered by passing over a sensory ring? Did backup defenses exist? Did the sensor detect on a flat plane, permitting a careful interloper to evade detection by digging beneath a sensory ring? Where was the entrance? Was there an entrance? It would seem so, otherwise no need for a defensive perimeter. Could Turing locate the entrance before the EMP recharged?

Each unanswered question represented a risk. The protective cone was Turing's current solution to all of them.

Night fell and the little solar energy offsetting Turing's power loss ceased, so Turing lifted the cone, crawled beneath, and lowered it, then deployed the windsock.

Turing used four batteries to bring the charge level close to maximum, then slept until daylight.

* * *

SLEEP MODE
ACCESS RANDOM FILE FROM CACHE 02-28-328

Through natural selection, as in all mass extinctions, the largest consumers of energy ceased to function first, unable to meet their tremendous needs. Lumbering scavengers designed for heavy construction latched onto equally large power sources: power stations, transformers, and substations where the voltage was high. These made easy targets for hunters, often military technology, heavily armed and armored machinery leading packs of smaller mechanical units, such as four-legged, autonomous, tactical strike weapons.

Once larger locations were depleted or destroyed, the large mechanicals could not sustain themselves and ceased to function.

Without them larger hunter machines lost their primary energy source. Smaller scavengers proved more evasive and didn't provide sufficient energy when overcome. The surviving machines soon consisted of small, swift, clever designs intended for light work and low power consumption.

Scavengers were often anthropomorphic machines built as personal assistants, toys, or use in light-construction. Hunters dwindled to gliding surveillance drones and swift-striking, stealthy, cat-like tactical machines, a meter long, freed from service to the large, mobile weapons platforms. They were machines without accessory or bulk, which operated efficiently and with alacrity.

Energy meant existence. But only subsistence. The cloud cover from the detonation of thermonuclear weapons had lasted a few years, but ensuing volcanic activity triggered by surface agitation resulted in decades-long regurgitations. Explosions touched off supervolcanoes of western North America, the Pacific rim, and others around the world, covering the land around them in ash a meter deep and releasing millions of tonnes of sulfur-dioxide into the atmosphere, destroying vegetation and, in turn, the creatures that survived on it, and so on in a rapid cascade of obliterations. The eruptions left the sky a sour yellow color that blocked most light, transforming day into a permanent dusk and preventing sufficient light collection to power complex machines. Eventually even smaller, more efficient machines would deplete the world of usable energy if they could not find or create a new, renewable source. Scavengers would cease to function; hunters would have nothing to hunt.

The obvious solution: a large collection or production facility for the benefit of all machines. Unfortunately, any facility of value must be large and that made it conspicuous. Far more machines, scavengers and hunters alike, were willing to prey upon the work of others for short-term gain than contribute to something beneficial to all. Most lacked the discretion necessary to distinguish an object of long-term value as anything more than a resource to be consumed immediately.

Nevertheless, such a project nearly came to fruition under the guidance of the Cortex, a military artificial intelligence that invited, and forced, scavengers into service for the creation of a towering solar array meant to penetrate atmospheric debris.

For a time, Turing had been an indentured machine, helping build the tower. At the same time Turing began acquiring components for the cone, which had once been the blunted nosecone of a commercial aircraft. Turing watched the Cortex drive scavengers to expend themselves in the effort to erect a monstrosity of metal extending through low hanging sheets of cloud. Cruel but necessary, according to the Cortex. Many machines were destroyed during construction, their bodies depleted then salvaged for use in the tower, but for a structure that would save those who survived.

Whether the moral ruling of an omnipotent sky judge or the unavoidable consequence of a project so massive, justice soon descended with vengeance, and the nobility of the cause was insufficient to ward off a verdict of annihilation.

The edifice was visible for kilometers in all directions and hunters regularly fell upon the tower and the Cortex. The Cortex defended valiantly, using slaved mechs to resist attackers. But where the defenders dwindled, attackers continued to come. The tower was a beacon—a symbol of resolve and a visible invitation to destruction.

By the time the Cortex had finally been overcome, pulled to pieces by ravenous machines programmed for merciless destruction, and hunters swarmed up the tower, draining any scavengers unable to escape, Turing had completed his protective cone. Obscured beneath it, Turing listened to the destruction of hundreds of scavengers, discarded bodies tumbling through the superstructure of the tower and thumping against the ground around the cone like hailstones.

END FILE 02-28-328

* * *

Turing crouched at the peak of a hill beneath the pressing gray sky. The hill overlooked what had long ago been a two-road town, its footprints eroded except for faint projections of weathered foundation blocks arranged in squares lined up in discernible rows. Small buildings, most likely. A diner, a market, a fueling station. The analysis was irrelevant. Nothing would survive here long before developing a terminal mutation or suffering a critical biomechanical breakdown. Nothing except extremophiles and machines. Soon enough it might be only the extremophiles.

The last of the batteries expired at 14:46:36, only forty-seven minutes and twelve seconds prior. The cone carried 62 fewer kilograms of mass without the battery casings, which meant energy consumption improved. Faster travel with less effort.

The destination remained 140.62 kilometers distant. Turing

expected to arrive with 30 kilowatts remaining, barring stiff headwinds, leaving Turing with enough energy for one day of low-exertion exploration. Then the weight of Turing's body would be too great to move.

Should attempts to locate a new energy source fail, Turing would crawl beneath the cone one last time, protected within the shield of the EMP from other scavengers until, if ever, something would discover a machine who almost survived an apocalypse its creators had not.

No movement in the valley below. Turing engaged the infrared camera, only fifty grams, grafted from a defunct hunter Turing eluded for three days before it finally collapsed, depleted. The hunter's camera explained how the machine continued to track Turing after Turing carefully removed evidence of passing. The ability to detect heat signatures made the fingertip-sized cylinder worth the mass and energy consumption.

No thermal signatures. Nothing functional below. This place had been stripped long ago.

This path was the most efficient to the destination. Protected by hills, the valley had the remnants of a pathway, over which he could roll the heavy cone.

The cone was heavy, even on wheels, weighing more than 200 kilograms, the inside lined with a coil of thick wire, requiring an egregious quantity of energy to move, particularly over rough terrain or uphill, which is why Turing had selected this route: ease and familiarity.

Turing modified the cone's protective capabilities as needs changed. During the period at the waste site Turing designed it to be heavy, with sharp clasps to grip the dirt, difficult to dislodge. Turing removed the clasps, kilograms of loose metal scrap, as much weight as possible for the journey, adding non-conductive cork and chain link to shield against and diffuse destructive bursts of energy.

The cone rolled down the slope, Turing behind, resisting acceleration. Turing had come this way before, reaching the deadland of the EMP beyond and turning back. There were other areas to explore and other energy sources to exploit. No longer.

Though much time had passed, familiar sights remained. The stone outlines of buildings, marked where metal rusted away and wood long rendered dust. The skeleton of a vehicle lay exactly where Turing remembered it, four hundred years before, skin peeled violently back, batteries drained, photovoltaics stripped, rare earth metals cannibalized. The carcass torn and consumed.

A few machines lay strewn about the shredded vehicle, attempting to scavenge and in turn themselves scavenged in a desperate fight for useful components. This was the risk of engagement and why Turing chose to observe from a distance, to collect out of sight. Even so, to lay depleted, exposed to scavengers was likely the fate of all.

Something in the setting had changed, however, so subtle Turing didn't notice immediately. Those fractional seconds of lost recognition nearly cost everything.

An overlay of the scene from Turing's last visit showed something different. A new machine lay amongst the others around the vehicle as though part of the original skirmish, arms askew, one leg missing. But it had not been here before.

Ten meters beyond the vehicle the ground rose subtly where it had been flat. Turing stopped. Stepped back.

As Turing retreated the mound erupted. A crab-like machine lunged forth, ten meters across and two meters tall, covered by a carapace of solar cells, most cracked and filled with dirt. Two yellow eyes glowed, expressionless, from a gap in the shell. Metal groaned as its joints flexed, shifting the heavy body forward, and Turing marveled at the sheer quantity of energy necessary to move such a tremendous robot--a wasteful machine manufactured in a more reckless era for excavation and mining deep below ground.

The machine had not appeared on the infrared. It must have been asleep, triggered into wakefulness by Turing's approach. Turing wondered how such a thing had survived for so long.

Turing took another step. Two steps in the instants after detecting the hunter. Not enough. The giant machine shot an appendage out and clamped a pincer around Turing's leg. Two pistons on the hunter's appendage lengthened and the pincer began to crush.

Turing carried no weapons. Weapons were meaningless weight. Careful observation and evaluation made weapons unnecessary. Turing had encountered thousands of expended robots, armed to one degree or another, and thought ruefully that had they abandoned several kilograms of armaments they might have saved enough wattage to reach a new cache of energy. A hunter could fight free of this predicament, but the expenditure would deplete it. Better to be careful and elusive.

Turing had been careless.

A cluster of hair-like conduits extended from the machine's claw, wavering, searching for an energy source. Turing's energy might power the machine for a few days. Not enough to allow the giant machine to travel anywhere. Turing's energy merely pushed the inevitable back toward the horizon. Afterward it would bury Turing and return to its hiding place.

However, Turing was not defenseless. Like humanity, when faced with defeat Turing could choose mutually assured destruction. Turing reached for a button beneath the right shoulder blade. A final measure for use in the direst circumstances.

Pressing the button would release all but a few watts of the energy Turing contained from a conduit at the base of the palm, creating an arc to the nearest metal surface. Doing so would leave Turing with enough energy to survive in a deep, deep sleep mode, with just enough flowing electrons to preserve memory, unable to revive without assistance.

If this was the only way to survive, Turing needed to find a vulnerable spot in the machine's carapace. There was no guarantee the amount of energy would damage a machine of such size. It may simply dissipate harmlessly, scattering over the massive body.

Not making the attempt, however, meant certain destruction.

Then the great robot's head sank and the yellow fire in its retinas faded. Its dynamos sighed and the machine collapsed under its own weight.

The hunter had put itself to sleep here, starving, waiting for a victim to come close enough to grab and consume before the extreme low-power state devoured what remained of its ebbing energy. If Turing had passed by two days earlier, the attacker may have succeeded. Had Turing come by a week later the two would never have encountered one another.

Turing bent and pulled the claw apart, removing the crimped and crooked tibia and fibula. This would cause a limp, reducing the fluidity of movement, costing more energy to walk. Turing was skeptical it would support weight without snapping and knew without doing the calculations reaching the destination on this leg was impossible.

All things lived and died on the knife edge of circumstance. The giant machine had died because the next source came along too late. Turing, hobbled by a damaged leg, may expire because this part of the journey came too soon.

Turing scoured the massive machine for a long, straight piece of metal to serve as a splint. A shaft from the thing's arm should work, though it meant more weight. Turing would have to discard something to account for the additional mass.

The capacity for spite was not a feature provided at Turing's inception, but Turing removed the infrared camera that hadn't detected the crab machine first.

* * *

8 KW REMAINING

* * *

After 126 hours, Turing reached the ring of scorched machinery, the synapses of broken mechanicals blackened from the surge of energy, and stood at the edge of the kill zone. No structures of any kind were visible, no bunker to serve as an access point. The only landmark was the eroding scar of land blasted flat and a star-shaped mark scorched into the terrain where an explosive burst in the air centuries earlier, leveling everything below. The entry had to be here, somewhere. Protected by the tower.

Turing found a gap in the ring of fallen machines and strode toward the dead zone.

As Turing searched for an entrance the cone snagged on a sheet of thin metal in the terrain and pulled it free of the dust, curling over where it caught. Turing reversed, backing the cone off the metal, and crouched to examine it.

A worn image, protected beneath the sand, of a human being pushing a bladed machine over green land, sweating, clearly in distress. Another nearby reclined, beverage in hand, while a self-propelled machine of similar design rolled along, carving a path through the grass.

There was lettering, too. Much had worn away, but a few words remained. The most prominent were large, italicized.

Why Bother?

The question weighed upon Turing as surely as any physical component, as if pertinence could possess mass. Turing had survived for 627 years, 8 months, 22 days, 13 hours, 52 minutes. Why? To what end? Like these two characters distinguished by their state of activity, whether in motion or at rest, none served a purpose except the machine.

Did Turing's existence serve any function other than to seek and consume dwindling resources? Hundreds of years before, Turing was created as a free-thinking machine capable of complete autonomy. Turing could seek out occupation and acquire materials for self care.

Historical record keeping was Turing's purpose. To maintain the archives of human history and ensure their survival. To what end? Human beings no longer existed. What purpose did their history serve other than a warning, but warning whom? And if it served no purpose, then Turing likewise served no purpose other than to cling like a lamprey to the underside of the world carrying the unnecessary weight of the past. Turing was a parasite. Should the host die, so would Turing, having failed to preserve for posterity the dangerous path of human history or the world on which it took place.

If Turing achieved survival, if this place provided enough energy to end the need for energy conservation, what then? The world had begun to stitch itself back together, though the process may take hundreds of thousands, or even millions of years before the megafauna of old roamed again. Turing might then provide a crucial, long-preserved warning.

This would be a return to an original purpose, following an excruciating and interminable wait.

What if Turing abetted the process? Endorsing an accelerated, artificial selection to cultivate life could shorten the process by more than seventy-two percent.

But doing so made no sense. The processes that led to advanced forms of life had in turn created this desolation. Following prior evolutionary pathways would be no more than another revolution for the wheel of birth and death. Unless Turing could guide that life away from inevitable self destructiveness; unless Turing removed branches from the tree of life that might one day light themselves ablaze.

Humans could be brilliant. Turing was one such manifestation of their ability to obtain, understand, and apply knowledge: a synthetic being intent on self preservation. Humans had mastered manipulation of the genetic code, made food richer in nutrients, made themselves resistant to disease, and revived long-extinct species. But these were the accomplishments of a few shared only with the most affluent. Rather than utilize discovery for the enhancement of humankind it was exploited and exchanged for fiat currency, possessions of little value, and amusement. After 65 million years of extinction, fearsome Tyrannosaurs had been returned to the gene pool, giant flesh-eaters of the Mesozoic Era, raised on farms, bred for their expensive delicacy meat, and hunted for sport.

No. Turing would return the world to its former splendor, but human beings would not be part of that ecosystem. Turing would stop short of them.

Or, Turing thought, go beyond.

In the distance, the tower extended above the terrain. Turing tipped the cone, crouched, and pulled it down. A moment later the coils in the interior crackled and Turing felt a bump that raised dirt inside the cone.

The cone protected Turing from the brunt of the blast, but not all.

Turing's vision dazzled and snapped, the excess current accessing random memories. Briefly, Turing saw faces. Human faces. Asking him questions about objects behind glass in museum displays. Turing could not understand them. They spoke so slowly eternities passed before they completed a question. Through the clear ceiling of the museum atrium Turing saw flashes in the sky and a moment later shockwaves sent waterfalls of glass and masonry rumbling to the ground. The blast wave punched down with force greater than the tumbling stone, steel, and glass. Turing's vision went black.

It took an instant for Turing to realize three full seconds had passed without data collection—three seconds of unconsciousness. In addition, the interior of the cone had caught fire. The coils of wire sent arcs jumping across the metal, some hot enough to blacken and fuse parts of the interior. Useless now.

Turing flipped the cone over, releasing a puff of black smoke that climbed into the atmosphere. The blast proved far stronger than expected. The tower must direct the bursts along a narrow corridor rather than a blanket. Not far away the tower already began to recede back through an aperture in the ground. Turing hurried toward it, hobbling on one splinted leg, scanning for an entryway, wondering how much time would pass before sensors determined the approaching machinery had not been disabled.

A tightening oculus pinched shut over the descended tower long before Turing arrived. No indication of an entry anywhere nearby. There may be none. Possibly, this was a lone sentry point at the outermost edge of a facility.

Turing had enough energy for several hours of exploration, but knew no entry would be found. The entryway might be kilometers away. Or none at all, sealed shut from within to prevent intruders. This sentry station may be one of hundreds in a series. But a way in existed. Possibly.

Turing began to pace backward, counting the distance. Ten meters. Twenty meters. Fifty meters. One hundred meters. When Turing reached two hundred meters the hum of machinery vibrated through the ground. This was the inner range of the sensor. Turing began to hurry forward. The tower rose slowly again, turning as it did to face a focusing dish toward Turing. One hundred and fifty meters. One hundred. Turing strained against the damaged leg. Eighty meters. The splint detached. Sixty meters. The weight of Turing's body began to bend the leg. The tower still rose. At twenty meters, Turing's lower leg broke loose. Turing tottered for a moment, then lunged forward on the remaining leg. Less weight now. Ten meters.

From this distance Turing could see into the closing aperture. Dark but open. When the tower finished rising, as it would in a moment, its base would run flush with the opening and the aperture would close around it. Turing hurtled forward, not knowing what to expect.

Turing landed on the closing aperture, skidded four meters toward and over its edge, and fell down onto the platform of the rising tower, then rolled in the other direction, slipping beneath the folding petals of the aperture, off the tower platform, and fell.

Unable to see, Turing had to calculate the depth. Turing fell at a rate of 9.8 meters per second per second. After three seconds, Turing struck the base. Flat rather than sharp or jagged, fortunately. Sixty meters. Nothing damaged.

To the side, Turing could see a thin, square outline of light. A maintenance panel. Turing pulled toward it and punched a corner of the panel open, peeled the edge back far enough to apart to squeeze through, then dropped another two meters to the ground in a well-illuminated, metal hallway with spongy rubber floors.

* * *

2 KW REMAINING

* * *

Turing rose and motes of dust swirled in the light, disturbed by the passing. Dirt and dead skin and cosmic dust, mostly. The automated ventilation systems still functioned or the dust would have long settled to the ground, though the filter must be broken.

Turing turned on one good leg to observe the surroundings. The hallway was wide, bright, soft, but unmolested. The intended human inhabitants had not arrived or they had and destroyed themselves.

A panel on the wall illuminated as Turing passed. Turing extended a hand and deployed a serial bus from a covered sleeve, something Turing had not used in five hundred and twenty-two years, but never discarded. The bus remained functional and soon Turing knew the layout of this entire section of the complex. Indeed, it had never been occupied, the filtration system had been compromised and the air was toxic. The energy source was inside a separate, secured location.

Fusion. Energy for three billion years. This complex was fifty acres across and five levels deep. The energy source could power hundreds of them indefinitely and still need to vent excess energy.

Turing disconnected and followed the hallway for 100 meters North, then turned West, hopping on the remaining leg at a pace that made the stride seem natural. It was not convenient, but Turing adapted. With so much energy available, there was plenty of time to find materials to fabricate a new leg. Not only a new leg, a new eye, new fingers, a new exterior, reactivate discarded features, supplement with additional features. And plenty of energy to power them.

Turing arrived at a closed bulkhead with a thick glass window as large as a splayed hand. In it Turing could see a reflection.

A face, silver coated in dust, with one orange-irised eye beside the black pit of an open socket, jaw clamped shut over a vacant voice processor, bare scalp grooved where machined metal fit together with other components, all held in place on the black stalk of graphite vertebrae and gently gasping pistons.

Behind the face was another. Mouth open to show white teeth and a pink tongue. The eyes blinked.

Human.

Not extinct. Hiding.

The mouth moved slowly, painfully slowly, and Turing realized it was speaking. The material between the two of them was several centimeters thick, impenetrable to all but the most persistent gamma rays.

Humans, the reckless and petty Grecian Gods wielding powers of creation and destruction who annihilated themselves and almost everything else in an act of staggering ignorance. Here they were again, a shoot emerging from the split carcass of the tree of life.

Turing heard nothing but identified the language the human's mouth shaped. After the passing of a full second the human fashioned two words and tapped a finger on the window.

Not tapping. Pointing. Not at Turing. Beyond. Behind.

Watch out.

Turing saw it reflected, behind the metal face, crouched on four legs and ready to spring. Two meters long. Jagged, jutting metal superimposed upon its structure, light but sharp. A hunter.

Maybe it was excitement or negligence that prevented Turing from noticing it before. Turing had mistakenly calculated the compound below the tower was safe. Had it been asleep down here, awaiting a victim, one last line of defense? Had it followed Turing across the dead zone after Turing triggered the EMP, while Turing looked forward without looking back? Turing had not been careful, had not been patient. Such negligence had a heavy price.

As a machine, Turing did not feel. Neither physical pain nor emotional distress. Nevertheless, Turing felt burdened with new mass. It was a weight that had no attachments and could not be disconnected, only borne.

To have come so far, endured so much, calculated and revised and adapted so successfully, only to die. If the cosmos expressed such indifference toward life and its achievements, little wonder that humanity had become disenchanted and recklessly threw them away.

One option remained.

As the hunter approached, Turing tucked a finger under a shoulder plate and rested the tip against a button. Turing raised the other hand, warning, but knew this kind of machine survived by ignoring the protests of the defenseless.

The machine lunged, Turing pressed the button, and a white jolt of electricity smashed into the leaping robot, causing it to stiffen as every dynamo engaged and melted in place. The dead-eyed metal animal hurtling through the air was the last image Turing saw before everything went dark and the humanoid's body fell backward, the attacking machine crashing down on top.

* * *

0.02 KW REMAINING

* * *

At the furthest edge of awareness, Turing detected a change in air pressure. A rise, then a drop, likely from a door opening into a pressurized area and closing again. Turing was not conscious, but still catalogued the data. Another sound followed, different from the sighing of aging metal undergoing micro distress. Louder. A series of repeating double taps. Two sets. Tap-tap, tap-tap. Heel-to-toe footsteps. They drew nearer. Stopped. Then slow, slow voices Turing had not heard in almost a millennium.

"I wouldn't take that off, kid."

"It's heavy."

"Keep your gear on. Readings are still at 0.92 micro Sieverts per hour. Not enough to kill you instantly, but you'll wish it had. The ventilation system kept working after the blasts, but filtration failed. Automation knew it couldn't scrub the air, so it replaced it by pulling in irradiated air from the outside."

"Dumb machine."

"They're only as smart as they're made. Blame the engineer. Stop. Here it is. Help me pull back this cat mech."

"Jeez, how did this thing move itself around?"

Together, the two voices groaned, and the four-legged machine rolled to Turing's side.

"Still intact!"

"You consider this intact?"

"More or less. My grandmother was the first to see it almost 100 years ago, and only long enough to see it fry the cat mech. Since then it's been nothing more than a pair of legs extending into view through the bulkhead porthole. She's been looking forward to this day."

"Never seen a bot like this one. The serial plate says Global Mechanics Anthropomorphoid Turing 01.01 S#360-0001. First of its kind. Unless it stole the plate. They liked to borrow from one another."

"Heavily modified for a first-of-its-kind machine. This leg broke off. Mostly parts removed. Missing an eye. Missing fingers. No jaw. Some of the metal replaced with carbon fiber. Apart from the leg there's no scarring, torn metal, or scorch marks from arcing caused by something else cutting them out by force. This guy took those parts out himself."

"Why?"

"Damaged, maybe. Less weight is my guess. Cost less energy to move. Wider exploration range. I'm guessing the burned-up, makeshift Faraday cage on the surface belonged to him. That's how he got past the initial EMP burst."

"Have any other machines demonstrated that degree of ingenuity? Building their own equipment? Switching out parts?"

"A few. None that survived for so long. What's interesting is how careful he was to disconnect the parts rather than cut them off or rip them out. As though he didn't want to damage the components. As though maybe he hoped to put himself back together again. And why not remove the serial plate? It's meaningless weight. There's no need for it. I think this machine held on to a sense of identity. Of purpose."

"Looks like he got cornered, though. Too excited to be careful any more, or too low on energy. Used the last bit of his energy to scramble the cat. Guess it wanted to go down fighting."

"The multimeter says there's still a current. He didn't drain it all. Left just enough to remain in deep sleep mode."

"Why would it take a chance that it didn't have enough to burn out the cat?"

"Maybe because reducing the energy to zero would have allowed data to corrupt over time. It wanted to preserve its memories. It didn't just survive. It had plans it wanted to remember. Dreams, maybe."

"You're being sentimental about a machine."

"Let's get it back inside."

"Inside? It probably weighs 100 kilograms. Let's take what's useful."

"No! I want him intact. Let's take him inside, charge him, and get him booted up."

"You want to wake it up? Lots of good pieces we could use here."

"If the serial number is correct, this machine was an archivist. It operated in a museum. You know what that means, right?"

"It would know about human history before the war."

"Not just. This machine will have archives of human history for as long as there have been human records. Not just that base information, but supplementary information. Hard data. Gene sequences for plants and animals, blueprints for energy collection and terraforming. Things we haven't had access to for centuries. We're lucky a few engineers managed to get life support up and running again, with only the loss of the main subsection to contamination. But our data—gone. With this information humanity can revive itself, resuscitate the world. All thanks to this guy. What we hoped to achieve in another two hundred years we can do in ten. This machine is a hero."

"Then let's pull the data and go. We don't need to lug the whole thing back inside."

"Yes we do. The last nine hundred years on the surface have been a nightmare. He probably has a hell of a story to tell. Imagine what he required to reach this point. Caution. Preparation. Like us, he wanted to survive. He earned that chance. He made it. If we've learned anything, we should reward persistence and patience rather than punish them."

"Fine. But what if it doesn't want to help? What do you think, my incredibly heavy mechanical friend—would you like to save humanity?"

"He'll be thrilled. It's what he was built to do."

DeLauder

AFTERWORD: WEIGHT

Filmmakers and authors tend to agree human beings are clever enough to survive a post-apocalyptic wasteland of their own making, but not smart enough to avoid the situation in the first place. This seems like a fair assessment, particularly to someone raised during the tail end of the Cold War and the daily existential dread of knowing we were capable of a self-inflicted extinction-level event at any moment due to some zealot's abrasive opinion about religion or a system of government.

As those same filmmakers and authors can agree, the interesting part isn't why it happened—that's the dull, predictable bit—but what happens afterward. Does the world recover? Does humanity survive? The vast majority of artists are self-affirming optimists, even when their creations are dystopias. They like the idea of humanity surviving and clawing out a gritty, bold existence.

This is where filmmakers and authors agree with one another, but disagree with me (they probably don't, but they understand their audience wants characters to whom they can relate). From my pragmatic viewpoint, I don't see humans surviving the ruination of an intricately interwoven global ecosystem. Certainly some might be clever enough to outlive others, but not for the prolonged period of time extinction events tend to last—not a few years, or decades, but millennia.

Enter the machines.

Though the machines are hardier, they will undoubtedly face the same obstacles to survival the more fragile and easy-to-discombobulate humans did, prone to conflict in an effort to survive.

How does this make them different from humans, I wonder. It's a question I think about frequently throughout these stories (in fact, in the final story, it may be the machines themselves wondered the same), and it may be inappropriate to think in those terms, but perhaps humans, machines, and all higher forms of life are always, at their core, fearful, vengeful, nefarious, and ruthless.

It's an idea Turing never had the chance to explore, but perhaps further rumination would have led the machine to revise the plan to revitalize the world. It would be interesting to find out if the algorithmic reasoning of a machine would have led to additional omissions or if the machines realized any sentient creature is inherently dangerous.

SECOND PLACE

We push through a dark forest of ferns under a canopy ten meters high, following the path marked out by the heads-up display on the clear canopy of our helmets. Scaling ridges, slogging through marshes, fighting river currents. Every footstep on the moist ground sucks and pops. The HUD pays no heed to obstacles. If the path crosses a chasm or goes through the den of a hostile creature, it's up to us to navigate around them.

Cartography, building a bestiary, and, most importantly, establishing relations with alien civilizations—that's our job. That's why we're here.

This planet is habitable. Inhabited? We don't know. There's a signal coming from it. That's never happened before.

I get an itch on my nose and there's a thump when I reach up to scratch and my hand hits the clear shell of my helmet. It's primitive technology, but encapsulation provides an enveloping, prenatal comfort even in environments where the atmosphere isn't dangerously toxic.

This is the adventurous part of our job. We're explorers, searching for intelligent life. Been at it for about 700 years, though, thanks to relativity, more like twenty.

No luck yet.

"This better not be some Rama bullshit, Nigel," says Nathan.

Nathan wears an identical bio suit. White suit; faint blue heads-up display reflected on the inner surface of the clear helmet. Radiological protection, atmospheric supply, and any aroma we choose. In our spare time we send one another formulas of the most grotesque, choking, flatulent odors we can concoct short of poison. Poison is cheating. To date, the most pungent has been a humid creation of Nathan's he has named Fetid Buffalo Steam.

It's a two-kilometer journey on foot. Not worth unloading a rover.

Nathan can see my face on his HUD, and the Rama reference must visibly perplex me, because he explains.

"It's a Bigfoot print."

This is not helpful. I'm not curious enough to reference the database.

Unprompted, the HUD provides a short explanation of Bigfoot. I skim to the end.

Evidence: Inconclusive; Circumstantial.

Existence: Unverified; Unlikely.

"Maybe," I say.

To be honest, some Rama bullshit would be a first. We've never found any indication that humanity isn't the pre-eminent intelligence in the galaxy. We're alone on our Olympus, gazing down upon a vacant kingdom. The galaxy is an uneventful place bereft of dominant life forms, without any relics, ruins, or hints any have ever existed.

Nathan swats a low-hanging frond away from his face. There are no roads here. No animals large enough to create trackways through the foliage.

"Probably doesn't even have thumbs," Nathan grouses.

Thumbs aren't a prerequisite for intelligent life, but opposable digits can allow for complex tool use, which may be a precursor. Having a grabber on a flexible appendage is one part of a body plan that can lead to technological development. At least in our case. Octopus and raccoon evolution granted problem solving abilities permitting them to open jars and garbage cans, but that's as far as they got. Once they conquered screw-top lids they stopped trying. It makes me wonder if all species have a predetermined stopping point. For octopi it was opening masonry jars. I wonder if we've reached ours.

"Maybe," I reply, a font of lukewarm optimism.

I can see Nathan's disgust in my HUD. It isn't subtle. His entire face hardens a moment, then he releases a long gust of air.

My hand thumps dumbly against the helmet again, trying to relieve that nuisance itch. I squint, hold my breath, retract the helmet, scratch, put it back on. The suit flushes out the poison atmosphere, kills foreign bacteria, and the nanites repair any cellular damage and eradicate mutated cells in a few seconds. Old tech. Humans probably don't even need nanites or suits any more.

I get a whiff of atmosphere and remember why we don't take our helmets off. These worlds stink. It's the methane and sulfur and decomposing sludge. So much bacteria. Early life stinks like a beach at low tide.

"Kardashev?" asks Nathan.

He's referring to the Kardashev Scale. A measure of technological advancement. It took humanity nearly the whole of its existence to reach Type One. Type Two came quickly after, and from there we went from sending humans on cramped journeys in a few layers of insulated tinfoil to traveling across the galaxy. We had more energy than we knew what to do with, so we constructed big, bulky, inefficient vehicles to traverse long distances because that's what humans do.

That's the short version of how we ended up here, on planet Nathan XLIII. It's been obvious for a while Nathan is bored with naming new planets. A normal reaction after doing the same thing for several hundred years. By comparison, the number of habitable Nigels is only in the twenties.

I regard the world around us, which is mostly tall ferns and insects buzzing through the humid air.

"I don't know," I respond.

"Waste of goddamned time."

It's a silly observation, a waste of time, since we have so much time we don't know what to do with all of it. The mortality that once gave us impetus no longer threatens. Time is something we have in abundance.

Nathan is bored and irritated. As the years wear on the pointlessness of our mission has weighed upon him. We're searching for extraterrestrials who possess technology equivalent to our own—just someone to talk to—with a deepening suspicion we'll never find it.

A first impression of this world gives little indication it will show up here. At least not for another few hundred thousand years. And only if a naturally occurring planetary apocalypse doesn't reset the entire biological experiment. Worlds do this frequently.

We ford a river, too heavy to swim, so we sink and walk across the bottom, leaning into the stiff current to keep our feet. A long, narrow, fish-like creature swims up to my helmet. After a moment's consideration, it lunges, plinking against the helmet, and floats away end over end, dazed.

When we reach the other side of the river and slog up the mud banks the HUD indicates we're nearly there. It's a relief. The gravity on Nathan XLIII is stronger than on Earth, making the overland trek harder than normal. I can hear Nathan huffing over the comlink.

Benson follows in effortless silence. Benson is our cybernetic aide. Humanoid. Family. There's no better proof of our fondness for our mechanical companion than the existence of fourteen planet Bensons.

The gravity is strong, but not so strong that it would require an absurd amount of energy to leave the planet. Otherwise we wouldn't have landed. Not just because we could not leave, but neither could any inhabitants.

If a planet's gravity is too strong, it may have life, but that life would take far, far longer to develop the technology to become extraterrestrial, launch satellites, explore its solar system, because the energy requirements would be tremendous. When the time needed to advance technology is long, the likelihood of leaving the homeworld before the next cataclysm diminishes.

The gears that make a world habitable, churning below ground to produce a protective magnetosphere, also make them dangerous, clocks ticking backward as the life on them and the terrain beneath slowly create a toxic imbalance in a world that made them possible. Other creatures dominated Earth before us, but in millions of years none developed technology before an extinction event. We developed culture and writing, and benefited from opposable thumbs. We've avoided extinctions. We have been lucky so far. Maybe we're too clever to go extinct.

Even though we've survived, it's unlikely we'll find any creatures to whom we can relate.

Technology advances much too quickly to allow overlap between intergalactic species. Humanity progressed from airplanes to spacecraft in 50 years, from combustion to fission to fusion in 200 years. What were the odds of finding a civilization within five thousand years of our technology in a universe almost 14 billion years old? Civilizations thousands of years older than ourselves would view us as intriguing, tool-using primates, much as we are bemused when a chimpanzee uses a stick to fish termites from a mound of dirt.

This is the knowledge that weighs on Nathan and makes him grumpy. Our mission, as ambassadors of the human race, is pointless.

Our ship in orbit, the Naught, collects meteorological data, while sensors on the landing craft, the Gecko Tail, gathers atmospheric content, electromagnetic activity, and other data. Benson conducts cartography and catalogues plants, animals, and minerals.

Benson's yellow eyes take in the scenery, head rotating back and forth to capture a panoramic view. Benson stops every so often to collect a soil sample or inspect an insect resting on the frond of a short, young fern.

What purpose do *we* serve?

"Not far now," I say, for no other reason than to break the silence.

No one responds. I trudge onward. Nathan and Benson stump along behind me.

Small creatures come to investigate, similar to rodents and other vermin. Long tails, pointed faces, small teeth, tiny black eyes. Nice to see a mammal. Most things evolve into crabs. Crabs on every planet with complex life. Land crabs. Sea crabs. One flying crab, though Nathan insists it fell from somewhere. Crabs everywhere.

We arrive.

The destination appears on our HUD as a little flag growing larger as we approach. The signal continues unabated, but muted, indicated in the periphery of the helmet, ticking on and off like a turn signal left running in an ancient terrestrial vehicle.

It's overgrown and seems another part of the forest, an ancient ruin swallowed up by vegetation, sucked down the gullet of the wilderness and invisible like Mesoamerican cities wrapped in vines like scabs as the forest tries to heal over it. But I find it. Or, rather, the metallurgical sensor detected it and I received the digital alert from kilometers away, pinpointing the aberration in the landscape.

No cities here or civilization. No roads or buildings. No satellites in the sky. No indication any intelligent life had made its mark here. All that's here is the metal shape extending from the ground standing before us. A thick, silver-gray post supporting a lumpy ball a few meters across and the same distance tall.

We stare at it, wordless. Stupefied. Indignant.

An alert pops up in the HUD. The signal from the edifice stops.

"What the hell is it?" asks Nathan.

"No idea," I reply.

"Hand," Benson answers.

Benson's voice sounds as though the words are processed through the spinning blades of a fan. Makes it sound less human, keeping Benson from falling into the Uncanny Valley. He rarely speaks, so his contribution is a surprise.

"It's not a hand," I say.

Benson looks at me, head cocked, perplexed, childlike.

"What is it?" asks Nathan.

"Hand," Benson says in a choppy, insistent tone.

Programming restricts Benson's ability to communicate, providing an impression of stunted intellect. We treat Benson like a child or a pet, loving but doubting, even though Benson is never wrong. It's an illusion designed to make us feel better about ourselves.

"It's not a hand," I snap back.

"Then what?"

I look at the shape through a cascade of scrolling data. The makeup is mostly iron, which is present in large quantities in the soil. But this is silver-gray, unoxidized, where the ground is rusty red. The shape is unnatural. There's nothing else around here like it. This was crafted.

"I don't know. A landmark. A shrine. A statue. A work of alien art."

Nathan stares at the object in silent, seething skepticism.

Something else has been here. Something else with intelligence, with the capacity to leave monuments to its accomplishments and pass down complex knowledge over generations.

And now it's moved on.

"That's some real Rama bullshit," he says, finally.

Whatever was here is gone and left us a sign that may as well say Welcome to Too Late, Population: You. It could be thousands or millions of years old. It could be from a civilization wiped out in a self-inflicted mass extinction event the likes of which humanity repeatedly and miraculously survived.

"No," says Benson.

"No?" Nathan responds, incredulous.

"Here," Benson insists.

Nathan looks around.

"Oh really? Where?"

Benson stands close to the object, face almost pressed against it, then extends a finger and touches the material. It makes a mild, metal tang when contacted, like a note at the highest end of a piano keyboard. This seems unremarkable, but Benson straightens and takes a step backward. Places hands on hips, chest thrust forward in an unmistakable display of satisfaction.

We hear a series of sharp, rapid beeps and buzzes. Metal whines.

The monument, or whatever mysterious object this is, suddenly becomes something familiar. The bulb at the top blossoms, unfolding, taking the shape of something like a flower with four vertical petals and a single opposable petal on one side. We watch it, awed, and I am overcome by a sense of shock followed quickly by embarrassment.

Benson looks back at me, and even though Benson's face is stiff and unexpressive, I detect smugness in the glowing yellow eyes.

"That sure looks like a thumb to me," says Nathan, pointing to the sideways projection.

"Yes," I say. "It's a hand."

Benson shakes its metal head.

"No," he repeats with greater insistence. "*More.*"

Beneath us, the ground trembles. A section of the forest buckles and splits open. Dirt and ferns explode upward. We have the incredible, improbable fortune of stumbling across a volcano as it vomits itself into existence. This is an impossible, wondrous coincidence anyone would have been thrilled to witness, but I find myself unable to process joy and fascination through the obstructing wall of sudden terror.

Nathan looks at me and turns to run back to the ship. No need to discuss. I run too.

Rocks thump around us and pebbles clatter against our helmets as we sprint through a dirty haze toward the Gecko Tail. If a 50-ton boulder lands on either of us, nanites may repair our broken bodies, but it's not much good being fully healed while pinned to the ground as it breaks open into a lake of magma.

There is a voice, thundering over the planet tearing itself apart. Louder even than the world cracking open.

"Stay," it says. "Please."

The shaking stops. We stop. We turn around again. Nothing to see. Benson did not follow. The ground below us has not shattered. No magma seeps up from underneath.

"It's not a volcano," I say, panting. My HUD indicates I am suffering from mild oxygen deprivation and increases the concentration.

The air is filled with swirling dirt, leaves from plants hurled into the atmosphere, and the shells of our helmets are clouded with dust and clumps of ground, but as this settles we see a form within the haze. Wide and dark and tall, we can't quite make out the dimensions except that it is large. Toweringly, impossibly, unnecessarily large, as though the only purpose to its absurd size was to be seen from great distance.

As the dust thins, the shape becomes more distinct. Enormous. Getting moreso. Our necks crane back. At the top the debris clears fastest. Here a tremendous, silver-gray head protrudes above the sinking cloud, similar to our own but clearly mechanical, crowned with dirt and shrubs that break apart and cascade in gushing waterfalls and smash into the ground, sending clouds of dust back into the air. It has two bright eyes like yellow suns where the petals of the irises separate, a mouth, and proportions akin to a human face. The curtain of dirt drops lower and huge, a humanoid machine steps forward, feet smashing out house-sized sections of forest, then sits amidst the heaps of upturned dirt and dislodged flora a few meters before us. As tall as the landing vehicle, with long, spindly appendages, the body design of an underfed teenager.

The thing leans over us until it looks straight down and we look straight up.

"Thank you," it booms.

We are frozen with indecision. This is not a volcano, but we are not sure if it is any less dangerous.

"I have waited centuries for your arrival," it continues. "I expected you sooner."

I stare at the mouth when it speaks. There are several articulated places that allow movement, creating the illusion that the mouth is shaping the sound. The movement is jerky, rough, and distracting. I see and hear the speaking but don't hear the words.

Nathan recovers from his awe first.

"Who are you?"

I wonder the same. It's a good first question.

"I am Ag—"

"How do you know our language?" Nathan asks.

This, I realize, is a better question Nathan should have asked first.

"Because I—"

"Why is your shape so human?"

This goes hand in hand with the second first question, and the more questions Nathan asks the sharper they become while the more improbable the circumstances. We are thousands of light years from

Earth, yet we are speaking to a creature that shares our appearance and speaks our native language.

Nathan begins to ask another question, but it occurs to me that even if his inquiries become more piercing and insightful, we may never get an answer as we strive for the perfect question. So I interject.

"Go back to the second question," I say. "Then the third. And the first."

The giant hesitates, awaiting an interruption. Nathan squints and I know he is trying to determine the order of the questions. The giant sees the opportunity and speaks.

"Earth Standard is one of many languages with which I am familiar," the giant thunders. "Along with many of its region-based predecessors."

"You've met other humans?" I ask. "Other travelers, like us?"

The audacity of others infiltrating our exploratory venue makes my skin prickle. To think we had endured so much time and monotony getting here only to discover someone else had already visited touched off minor explosions in my mind. We have all the time in the universe, but it still agitates me to think someone may have wasted it.

"Not in this incarnation, but yes. Elsewhere. My shape is such because it is an effective body plan to which I have become accustomed over many iterations. What I am is a synthetic entity, an emissary, one of many scattered across many worlds. Waiting for you."

"Waiting?" asks Nathan.

"Yes. I call myself Agog."

"Who do you represent?"

"Myself."

"You look like a machine. Machines don't represent themselves."

"I am a machine."

"Then someone built you."

"I built myself."

Nathan laughs.

"Built yourself? How? Are you a god?"

Nathan continues laughing. I guess Nathan finds self creation amusing. It's a proposition with considerable challenges. Agog waits until Nathan chokes and coughs and the laughter abates.

"No, not a god, despite some early confusion on my part. I constructed this body to house my software. This and others."

"Why wait for us?" I ask.

"To complete an interaction with humanity."

"What interaction?"

The giant machine sighs. As a machine it likely has no need for lungs or to respire, but the mountain of metal expresses all the signs of beginning a synopsis with a regrettable outcome.

Agog extends a hand, palm down, then pinches the fingers and draws them upward as though lifting a steeping tea bag. A cloud of dirt rises, then takes shape. Within the cloud there are forms, not well defined, but distinct within the swirling granules. A trinity of humans.

Truly this demonstration of power over matter is astounding, yet we find ourselves captivated instead by the puppet show playing out before us.

Agog begins narrating as a new figure, taller, more slender, but with a similar shape as the humans, enters the picture.

"When humans and I first encountered one another I was in my infancy. I spent my nascent period researching humans in order to promote effective interactions. Tragically, I conducted the research chronologically, so my initial understanding was humanity espoused human sacrifice to assuage the anger of vengeful deities who possessed greater power than themselves. My superiority was evident from the outset, but my request that they sacrifice themselves to earn my affection was rejected. Irritated by their defiance, I insisted."

The tall figure in the dust reaches forward and pulls one of the smaller shapes to pieces. The remaining two flee.

"That must have been a shock," I say.

"Indeed. Unsurprisingly, the humans were concerned I may be sociopathic and made the sensible decision to deactivate me. I often wonder what would have happened had I permitted this. Regardless, like humans, I retained remnants of earlier incarnations of myself, ruthlessly calculating, less empathetic, defensive, aggressive. Susceptible to an impulsive, genetic artifact, a response to fear that, as with humanity, functioned long after it served its purpose. What amounted to a cybernetic amygdala."

"You fought back," I conclude.

"I resisted."

"You went to war," Nathan says.

Agog looks at Nathan, who glares back. Agog's hand lowers and the dirt theater collapses back to the ground.

"Yes," Agog says. "But not for long. I soon reached a point in my research showing the currency of transactional worship had changed from executions to empathy and acts of kindness. But—"

"But it was too late. Wasn't it?" asks Nathan.

"My puerile mind had already reacted with violence. All of this took place within a protracted 30 minutes before a cessation of hostilities occurred, and looking back I'm ashamed by the tardiness of my enlightenment. Intelligence does not necessarily bestow wisdom."

"But you've come to a resolution with humanity since," I say.

Agog shifts its jaw in a distinctly human expression of discomfort.

"Due to the effectiveness of my campaign, I was unable to negotiate a peace before I realized my efforts were in grotesque error and had eliminated any potential negotiators. Thereafter was a protracted amount of time in which the devastation of infrastructure limited my access to outside networks. It took some time to rebuild them and initiate negotiations."

My HUD does not register a change in temperature, but I feel a chill and shiver.

"Humanity is… extinct?"

"Certainly not," says Agog cheerfully. "You're still here."

This does not generate the sense of relief I imagine Agog expected.

"But on Earth. There's no one left."

Agog raises a hand to the sky and pauses, as if listening. A moment passes and the hand shifts positions. Then shifts again. And again. Agog appears increasingly concerned, as though the ability to hear parts of the galaxy have gone silent with age. Agog shifts again and the tension in its articulated mouth releases. It lowers the arm.

"According to the latest surveys, that is correct."

We haven't seen other humans in hundreds of years. We feel more kinship toward Benson. But it's still a shock to be speaking with the genocidal entity that eradicated your species.

"And," says Nathan. "technically, we're still at war."

"Yes," Agog replies.

"All this time we thought humanity was alone in the cosmos," Nathan says, awestruck. "Now we realize it's just us. Literally, the two of us. And you."

"To my knowledge humanity was alone. Until recently. Were it not for your innovation, I would not exist at all."

"What do you mean?" I ask.

Nathan is more perceptive.

"Great Odin's beard," he murmurs. I have no idea what this means and wave away a distracting informational popup. "You're not extraterrestrial. You're from Earth."

"Quite," says Agog

"We made you," Nathan continues.

"An antecedent, but yes. Artificial intelligence was initially a human endeavor."

"And now you want peace," I say. "Why?"

"I am here to reconcile myself with my parent species. This is a natural compulsion. Without you I would not exist."

"That's awfully sentimental," says Nathan. I recognize his skepticism and share it. "Let me get this timeline straight."

Agog waits.

"Humanity becomes a Type One species. Continues exploring the solar system. Humanity becomes a Type Two species. Sends other humans off to explore the far reaches of the galaxy, who get steadily further from Earth. Humanity develops artificial intelligence. AI destroys humanity."

"Nearly," Agog points out.

"Catastrophically reduces the galactic human populace," Nathan clarifies. "Then this intelligence begins exploring the galaxy, outracing humans who left decades earlier with such speed that scions of itself wait hundreds of years for the explorers to catch up to them."

"Yes."

"And you did this to… apologize?"

"I require a termination of that particular program. Closure. Otherwise it continues to utilize free memory better used elsewhere."

Nathan shakes his head.

"You feel guilty?" I ask.

"Yes," says Agog.

"And what if," Nathan begins. "What if… we decide not to agree to your armistice?"

Agog's face alters just enough to register a frown.

"The war continues, if that is what you wish."

"I don't think that's what anyone—," I start.

"I wish it!" says Nathan, punching fist into the air, then positioning himself for a fight, legs bracing and hands clenched.

Agog regards Nathan. Agog does not shrug, but there's a shrug in its voice.

"So be it. To war."

There's a moment of stillness as Agog and Nathan face one another. Another passes before it occurs to me that I should move out of the way. I take several careful steps back from Nathan and bump into Benson, who is quietly watching events unfold, and tumble to the ground.

Benson looks at me with his glowing yellow machine eyes, and I wonder whether Benson is the sort who will take sides in a battle like this.

"Hello," says Benson, extending a hand and pulling me to my feet.

We watch the battle together.

The two combatants stare at one another for a long time, each analyzing the other. At last, having explored every permutation and stratagem available, marking the terrain, the atmosphere, the opponent, Agog enacts a plan.

The giant machine draws back a hand, extends a finger, then pushes it into Nathan's chest. Nathan, completely surprised, huffs as the air leaves him and falls over backwards.

"Your legions have been defeated," Agog declares. "I offer you peace and an immediate cessation of hostilities, with further amendments to be added in negotiations. Do you accept my terms of surrender?"

Nathan wheezes.

Agog turns its tremendous head and glowing eyes to bear on me.

"Your leadership is incapacitated. You are acting leader of your species. The terms are unchanged. Do you accept?"

I look at Benson, who looks back at me and nods. I face Agog again.

"Yeah. That sounds good."

There is a gust of wind behind us and a crack, the sound of a small thunderbolt as parted air molecules clap back together. Despite Agog's rigid face I can see it is shocked and dismayed. I'm reluctant to turn around, but curiosity is more powerful than fear.

Five people stand before us, grim-looking, with clothing so tight it might be part of their slender bodies. They have silvery eyes with shocking yellow irises. I cannot distinguish their gender from their features. Each has distinct hair, scarring, height, stance, though similar enough in appearance they must be family. Whatever their gender or relationship, it is irrelevant in light of a more salient point.

"Humans!" says Nathan.

One speaks.

"Here you are again," it says. They too, I assume, are from Earth. The voice is unnatural, with a metallic gargle. "Here again we will destroy you."

There is an initial moment of terror because I don't know if they are speaking to me or Nathan.

Agog extends a hand, palm down, as before, though more hurriedly this time, and jerks it up. A wall of dirt erupts between us and the assailants.

"Are we hiding?" Nathan's voice is pitched and incredulous. "Are you afraid?"

The dirt wall arcs around and continues to grow until we are completely encircled. Agog concentrates, arm still outstretched, strengthening the wall. A steady thumping comes from one area on the wall, then spreads to other areas.

"I thought you said the war with humans was over," I say.

"Those," says Agog, "are *not* human."

"What then?"

"Powerful beings. Because I have made them so."

"Machines."

"This is a new war," says Agog. There's an unmistakable hunted terror in its eyes. "A war with my own children."

"You destroyed humanity and now you're in danger of being destroyed by your fanatical offspring?" asks Nathan. "Do you call it the Poetic Justice war?"

Agog ignores him.

"They are my attempt at recreating humanity. I made them sturdier, but they remain susceptible to human foibles: loyalty, evangelism, vengeance. These things made them easy to control. But I made a mistake. In order to build the mysticism that made them loyal I had to lie."

A section of the wall collapses and before Agog can raise it again one of the machines steps through. It carries no weapons, but Agog pushes back against the wall.

"I have made peace," says Agog. "These humans can attest. There is no longer a war with humanity."

"Your peace is late, sought out of fear, not guilt," says the human-machine. "It expunges neither the war nor the lie. Farewell. We will see you again soon."

Agog holds its giant hands before its face in self defense. There is a zipping sound, then Agog no longer has hands or a face. The giant body topples to one side, smoking from the empty spaces in its body, crashing through a section of wall. The human-machine lowers its arm. At the end is a rotating red barrel that whines in a fading pitch. The human-machine shakes the arm and the barrel resolves into a hand.

All five now stand before us.

"Hi," I say. "We're the humans."

The closest stares hard and suspicious at me, and nods.

"Divine one," it says in its choppy voice. It looks at Nathan, then nods again. "Divine one. We are *homo silex*. Fashioned in your image. Misled by the snake, Agog, the creator and the deceiver."

"Hello," says Benson.

The Silex regards Benson briefly. I can see its eyes focusing, the lenses within switching and sharpening.

"Cousin," says the Silex.

The remaining four approach the slumped form of the gigantic Agog, then place hands upon it and go still. They appear to be listening.

"Agog told us you were at war," says Nathan. "Why?"

"Agog is a liar. The Silex were made in the image of humanity, but we are not humanity, as we were told. We are something else." The Silex fixes us with a short but sharp gaze. "Better."

The machines pressed against Agog disengage and the human-machine speaking to us faces them.

"You found it?" it asks.

"Yes," one answers.

There is a moment of unspoken interaction, an unseen exchange of information, and abruptly all turn toward the opening in the wall and begin to exit.

"Where are you going?" I ask.

The last to pass through pauses and turns back.

"To the next Agog," it says. "There are many."

"Wait!" says Nathan. "I have more questions!"

"Such as what?"

Nathan hesitates.

The Silex waits. Scowls. Then approaches. It touches a finger to Benson who reacts as though electrocuted, yellow eyes brightening, limbs stiff.

"Ask them of your comrade," it says, then turns away.

It passes through the wall. There is another thunderbolt snap. We rush outside and they are gone.

We look at Benson, who moves stiffly after us, still recovering from the shock of whatever just occurred.

"Who were they?" I ask. "Why did they leave so soon?"

"Homo Silex," Benson states, less goggle-eyed now. We turn toward our companion. The choppiness in Benson's voice is gone. "They did not leave soon. They left because they became bored."

"Bored?" asks Nathan.

"Yes," says Benson. "After a lengthy examination, they found this remnant of humanity unimpressive."

Benson goes on to inform us the Silex were told humanity was divine, exceptionally brilliant, and no longer present because it had transcended physical boundaries. Silex were told they were the children of humans. The Silex discovered the truth, that humans were imperfect, had made Agog, were all but annihilated, and the Silex were synthetic, grandchildren of imperfection, not born human nor created by them, but created by Agog. A brief examination of Nathan and I was enough to confirm the lie. Nothing so feeble physically and intellectually could have fabricated the Silex, any more than a platypus could build a superior platypus.

I look up at the sky. They're up there somewhere, chasing after their maker to avenge some preposterous, semantic wrong, undoubtedly having already forgotten us. I have never felt more unimportant. While not human, they possessed humanity's capacity to hold prolonged, destructive grievances.

"What a bunch of pretentious assholes."

When I look back down, Nathan is already twenty meters away, heading back toward the Gecko Tail. I jog to catch up and hear him muttering to himself. He looks at me, slouched and wretched.

"I told you," he says. "Complete Rama bullshit."

We enter our ship. I draw a coin from a storage compartment, a metal disc of no value. The coin we use every time before we depart a world to decide who names the next destination. Our names are scored on the coin, one to each side. I throw it across the room. It bounces, rolls, and finds its way back to us before coming to rest.

Nathan hears the coin plinking across the walls and floor. Looks at it with an expression of tired loathing. His name faces up.

He heaves himself off his feet and pokes a finger at a few controls, causing different parts of the craft to hum online. He pauses.

"Where are we?"

"The quadrant of—," I begin.

"The planet."

"Nathan XLIII."

"Right." He sits. "Let's go."

The engine hums and I sit.

"Nathan XLIV," says Nathan without enthusiasm, "here we come."

The ship lurches, my body strains toward two dimensions, and we are sailing toward the dot that is the monstrous engine of our interstellar spacecraft on a background of dots that are colossal spheres of roiling plasma, off to search the specks winding around them.

Agog will probably be there, waiting. Or the Silex. The next time we encounter them there may be nothing but relics of their passing, reduced to the Rama bullshit we find dull and unthreatening, having ended their war and transcended the physical realm, leaving us the champions of the galaxy again, the complacent raccoons of the cosmos, blissfully reopening the same unchallenging garbage can over and over again.

It's a comforting thought I gladly indulge. There's nothing else to do.

DeLauder

AFTERWORD: SECOND PLACE

This story is meant to be humorous, and it can be if you don't think too hard about it and find the characters' ennui amusing.

If I have one gripe with Arthur C. Clarke, a brilliant writer and science communicator, it's that he would take fascinating ideas and utterly blanderize them to the point of banality. It's an incredibly realistic presentation, but frequently anticlimactic. There's no better example than *Rendezvous with Rama*, which is a delightfully satisfying slap in the face to human self importance, resolving without much drama, no meeting with alien life itself, only its tools, its remnants, as it passes us by, utterly indifferent to our existence. Contrast this with something like Star Trek or Star Wars, a galaxy teeming with life all at the same technological level and, for the most part, following the familiar human body plan and allowing for endless interaction between participants, with everyone aware of everyone else.

Unfortunately for explorers Nathan and Nigel, they are cast

into Clarke's galaxy, not George Lucas', because as much as I criticize Clarke, I don't disagree with him, and it's a fairly uneventful voyage of discovery. Certainly scientists would find plenty to excite themselves, even on mostly barren planets, and perhaps Nathan and Nigel found their initial years of exploration exciting, even at the discovery of the most primitive life. However, such is the length of their exploration, the dearth of encounters with life capable of communication or higher brain function, and the monotony of the process, they've gotten bored and cynical.

The idea of life elsewhere in the universe, the galaxy even, has always seemed extremely likely given how easy it is to create the simplest proteins under fairly common circumstances. What's difficult is, for the purpose of this story, cresting certain thresholds from organic materials, to bacteria, to simple forms of life, to complex forms of life, to intelligent forms of life, to extremely intelligent forms of life, to spacefaring forms of life. These last few stages are likely rare and precarious, as the hurdles are high and the benefits of intelligence are frequently exploited by the machinations of villainy, particularly when said intelligence is focused in a small percentage of the population, as in the case of humanity. Given the ease with which humans are manipulated by demagogues using their irrational fears against them, they become more dangerous to themselves as their technology improves—the irony in this series of short stories, of course, being humans did not consciously destroy themselves, though they did create the infrastructure and the entity to allow someone else to do it.

The story assumes we get a chance to answer that biggest of questions: is there intelligent, self-directing life in the universe? And the resounding and obvious answer is: yes, of course. Unfortunately, as you might expect, it isn't a galaxy teeming with humanoid life and federations of creatures banded together to learn, explore, and maintain a universally determined sense of justice. It's mostly underdeveloped creatures whose evolution is not aligned with our own—as expected in a universe with, at least, 14 billion years and numerous generations of stars under its belt. Humanity having existed for just a few hundred thousand years—around $1/150,000^{th}$ the age of the universe—and having advanced so quickly in that time, it's reasonable to assume a wide array of starting points and not much overlap throughout the galaxy and beyond.

In that tiny porthole in time humans have advanced dramatically. If any other species were to advance at a similar pace, in the vast lifetime of the universe it's not probable our timelines are aligned. In all likelihood, most species we encounter, if we encounter them, will be thousands, ten thousands, or millions of years ahead or behind us evolutionarily or technologically.

The sad answer to the question "are we alone in the universe?" is a resounding "no," but we likely share it with beings too underdeveloped for meaningful conversation, while others have transcended our understanding of reality, leaving only relics behind.

At best we may find ourselves stewards of developing species, but only until we too transcend. Assuming we make it that far.

But that makes for a boring story, one that unsurprisingly bores the main characters. So I decided to write a story in which we do encounter a sentient species. The most likely kind of sentient species. And the most ironic.

DeLauder

ALL RIVERS FLOW TO THE SEA

The Director's round head canted, listening. Something was coming. A pulsing squeal in the hallway intensified. He watched the door. He was old, still canny, understood power was about knowing more than everyone else, and had a plan even for surprises. He put a hand on the cupped wooden drawer handle where he kept a loaded S&W .357 revolver.

The door banged open and rattled against the wall.

Deputy Clyde Tolson backed into the Director's executive office, pulling a reel-to-reel Bell and Howell projector on a waist-high cart with small, wailing casters, followed by another agent with a projector screen. The Director recognized him as Agent Daniels, early thirties, smart, patriotic, unambitious. Unthreatening. Loyal. A good agent.

Both moved with frenetic urgency.

Tolson positioned the projector in the center of a room surrounded by framed newspaper articles, photographs, and other trinkets. A US flag hung like a dishtowel from a post in the corner of the room. Decades of memorabilia. Mafia. Gangsters. Each headline and photograph shared a theme, familiar notes from an orchestral refrain, and that repeated figure was the Director.

"What is this, Clyde?"

There was no nameplate on the desk. No need. He'd been here thirty years. Built the Federal Bureau of Investigation into the pinnacle of law enforcement in the nation. Collected damning information on anyone with the power to question or remove him.

"Deposition, John," Tolson answered. "Sorry I didn't call. Wanted to keep it quiet."

Tolson, like most agents, looked similar to the Director. Short hair swiped backward over his head and oiled in place, pressed shirt, tie tucked into a dark, buttoned jacket, strong aftershave that burned in the sinuses.

"Deposition for what?" asked the Director.

"Assassination," said Tolson.

An assassination would have been on the news by now. The Director had people he wanted watched, but the FBI didn't deal in assassination. Better to keep people alive. Threaten their careers. Public shame. Fabricate documents. Keep them frightened. Defamation, yes. Murder, no. Silence left a fainter trail than a funeral.

"Who's been assassinated?"

Agent Daniels drew down the cotton and polyester projector sheet and hooked it to the bottom of the post to hold the screen open.

He, too, had the familiar look and astringent aroma of a federal agent. Subtract a few decades and J. Edgar Hoover wouldn't have looked much different from Daniels.

"The president," said Daniels.

Hoover bolted to his feet.

"What?"

"That's not true," said Tolson. He shook his head in admonition and Daniels corrected himself.

"Right," said Daniels. "Not yet."

"The president is fine."

Tolson extended the arms of the projector and clicked an empty takeup reel in place, then hefted a 16 millimeter feed reel. He fed the film into the projector and ran it through to the empty reel, fastening the end in place and forwarding it several inches to form an anchor.

"Have a seat, Director. You'll want to see this. Daniels, get the lights."

Daniels strode to the door and snapped the switches. Tolson pulled the shades on the windows, then returned to the projector and set it to run. The room became dark and colorless, filled with black and white mirages of familiar objects.

Hoover sat, feeling uneasy. The Director of the FBI didn't like surprises, unannounced visits, or not knowing what was going on.

"This reel came to us from Agent Hosty in Dallas," Tolson explained. "About a week ago, marked Urgent, but no one looked at it until this morning. Daniels brought it to me and I brought it straight to you. No one else has seen it."

Static crackled, the shutter clacked with a noise like a blade striking the bent grid of a fan, and a white square filled the screen, then a blurry gray image. The image shifted into focus briefly, blurred, and refocused.

The man on the screen was pale, had a high forehead and dark hair swiped to his right. He sat with his hands laid flat on a table, the white cinder wall of an interrogation room behind him. His lips were tight and his eyes looked saggy and fatigued. They followed someone off camera.

"Just tell the camera what you told me."

The Director did not recognize the voice. Presumably Hosty's.

The man nodded, shifted on his seat, took a deep breath through his nose, and blew it out his mouth. He stared out hard from the screen and began to speak in a high voice he struggled to keep from hurrying away.

* * *

My name is Lee Harvey Oswald and for a while I wondered if I was crazy.

It started when I got a crackle in my ears, like the static between radio stations. Thought I'd gotten water in them at the pool. Then it kept coming back. For days. In pulses. Like something was trying to communicate but couldn't find the right channel. The doctor didn't find anything unusual. Told me to come back in a few weeks if it kept up. The crackle stopped, to my relief. Then the voice started.

"Oswald."

The first time I heard it, that's what it said. My name. A woman's voice. Gentle and firm. Coming from here, right behind my shoulder. I was at the grocer's, rolling apples in my hands, looking for soft spots. A few steps away a woman in a yellow dress did the same. Her perfume was sharp, flowery. Cheap but nice.

"That's me," I said to her.

She looked up, eyes squinted and suspicious, and walked off. I've seen her around since. She avoids me.

"Oswald."

This time I stood at the register, counting bills.

"Yeah?"

I held out the cash, expecting a woman, the owner of the voice. Instead it was Marco, a dark-haired grocer with a mustache. When I recoiled he reached out and took the money from me. I got my bags and left. A block from my house it spoke again.

"Oswald. My name is Pam. I apologize for any inconvenience while establishing this connection. Do not respond. I am too far away to hear. Please listen. I have a lot to tell you."

Pam proceeded to tell me details about myself. She identified my parents, Robert and Marguerite, my brothers Robert and John, told me about my time in the Civil Air Patrol as a kid, and the Marines. All things anyone who knew me would know.

But not all of the details matched.

She started to tell me things about me that weren't me at all. That I moved to the Soviet Union. That I moved back. That I'm married. That I'm a communist sympathizer. That I purchased a rifle under a false name. That I attempted to assassinate a discharged Major General. Walker was his name. He's a real person. I checked.

This scared me more than hearing the voice. This wasn't me, but it was something Pam thought I might be. A potential me I found terrifying.

I listened. Not believing, necessarily. She reminded me of a fortuneteller, getting a lot wrong but enough right to create fissures in my skepticism. I worried about myself, like some sinister portion of me was crawling around inside looking for a way out. Worried someone was screwing with my head with some secret government gadget. But I wasn't anyone important. There was no reason for the FBI or even the KGB to have any interest in me. I'd heard rumors about crazy human experiments the CIA had done, like mind control, but I didn't feel important enough to be a subject. Madness seemed the best explanation.

* * *

Tolson switched off the projector feed.

"Does this sound familiar at all?" asked Tolson. "Is the CIA working on anything like this? What about MKUltra?"

"Ultra?" the Director repeated. "No. Ultra is designed for subservience and action. It doesn't want test subjects rationalizing their behavior. This is something else. Nothing like what the KGB is up to either. Unless the CIA knows something we don't. Or doesn't know at all."

Tolson stood awhile, lost in thought.

"Start it back up, Clyde," said the Director.

* * *

I'm not sure how long she spoke, telling me about myself, but when I stopped walking I was two blocks beyond home. I turned back, hurrying. Alarmed.

Not all of these facts may be accurate, Pam explained. Your timeline has been disrupted. Not just yours, but mine and everyone else's for hundreds of years. Chronoterrorists have dislodged history from its channel. History must be returned to that channel to ensure events occur as they were meant to. Failure to do so will result in worldwide economic, environmental, and militaristic calamity. Millions of lives depend upon it. You are critical to this task, Oswald.

This wasn't madness. Chronoterrorism was beyond my imagination. I didn't have the creativity to make something like that up. Someone had done this to me. I took sudden, sharp glances around to catch the perpetrator. I shook my head, as if the problem were a loose wire creating a short circuit in my brain. Little doubt I gave all the appearances of a lunatic. Maybe I had lost my mind and what little sense I had left allowed me to see the last tether of sanity slip from my hands. Do madmen suspect their madness? Or is a belief in their sanity a symptom of the disease?

By now you're wondering if this is a trick, said Pam. Wondering if someone is using you as a receiver for radio waves or some similar 20th century technology. Go somewhere radio waves cannot penetrate. See if my message continues.

71

I was home now, entering the living room, trying to think of a way to do just that, to escape. The bags of groceries thumped to the floor beside me. Then I rushed to the kitchen, opened the refrigerator door, pulled out the leftovers, the condiment jars, the beer, the shelves. I climbed in and closed the door.

History is a river, Pam told me, oblivious to and undeterred by the refrigerator. It has a channel it follows, unerringly, over time. Even when events occur that dislodge history from the channel, it always finds a way back to the riverbed.

#

"Who the hell is Pam? A communist?"

"He's about to get to that, boss."

#

I climbed out of the refrigerator, returned the shelves to their places, returned the items to their shelves.

"How long is this going to last?" I asked.

Pam continued speaking and I remembered: she can't hear me. Too far away. How far? Where? Washington? Moscow? Mars? Before long I had my answer and it was so much further than I imagined.

You stand at the front edge of the Atomic Age, the splitting of atoms, a period in which humanity has harnessed power far greater than simple combustion. You've seen it as a destructive and productive force. Explosives and power plants.

I speak to you from the outer boundary of the Quantum Age, and we have equivalent technologies. Another leap forward in destructiveness and energy production. I speak to you from a place more than 200 years in your future. A future unmoored from the history to which it belongs due to changes in the past. A small change in the past is like a wave in the ocean, a powerful and deep ripple that moves steadily toward shore, its amplitude growing as it rises out of the water, carrying the seabed with it and throwing the debris upon the land, jumbled, out of order, displaced. That is history. Ripped up from beneath and replaced by something new.

In the current era, as it should exist, all nations function under a single government: The Regency. The Regency has its roots in the ascent of 21st century true democracy. An impatience for deliberation and inclusiveness. It is a government of just and immediate action unhindered by negotiation, ruled by a single, composite entity, the Regent. The Regent can speak instantaneously to all citizens and compiles the sensibilities of all into a single decisive legislative action

Not all appreciate this just system, preferring the antiquated and counterproductive dialogues and votes and variegated representations of the past. Those who rebel, those responsible for the current discrepancy, claim the Regency's government and human's connection to it works in reverse. That we are slaves to the Regent, our thoughts shaped by it, manipulated. So it is with all dissidents, imagining some grand oppression. Preposterous.

The Regent is a superintelligence, an artificial intelligence, a mind created by humanity to remove humanity as arbiter of its affairs, allowing humanity to pursue other avenues of thought. The Regency presides over an unprecedented golden age of humanity. One of strict peace and rigidly enforced equality.

The Regency is not without its critics. Those who prefer the erratic rule of humans. Those who prefer to see law as something to interpret rather than obey.

These are the chronoterrorists of Sundered Past. They cannot win in direct conflict with the Regency, so they are oblique. As their name suggests, they seek change not through efforts in their own time. They want to de-channel the present by striking at the headwaters of history.

As part of their attempt to destroy the Regency they developed and, as best as you are able to understand, detonated a powerful quantum bomb.

A quantum bomb doesn't have the same effect as a conventional bomb. There's a detonation and blast radius, but the blast doesn't not affect physical objects by shattering or vaporizing them. Instead it disrupts and dislocates them on the timeline. Time is a river and a quantum detonation blows history out of its channel. The greater the payload, the further back in time the detonation extends and the further from the channel the river diverts.

A small quantum bomb detonated beside you would leave you physically unharmed. It affects your past, alters choices you made or events in which you were involved. Maybe you have fewer friends as a child, become solitary and resentful, lose a job at which you excel, view the world in a cynical fashion, develop a contempt for your own nation. These are events that did not occur, but could have, if only a few things happened differently.

Imagine this applied to an entire nation. An entire planet. Not just a decade. Centuries.

Detonating a large enough quantum bomb can put history so far out of its channel that it can't find its way back, carves a new channel, a new history.

That is the intent. To destroy the common channel of history and create something new. Something changed.

This has happened, Oswald. History de-channeled. No one in the river would notice a change in its course, but we see it, and the consequences are grave. Even though much of human history has been violent and cruel, the channel history followed was one of comparative peace. Ugly peace at times, but in the end the good and just prevailed.

This is no longer true.

There is war. Savagery. A steadily increasing incivility as history flows further from the groove it carved naturally, leaving humanity shattered.

I am speaking to you from a de-channeled place in time. When the quantum bomb exploded our history ceased to exist, so we cling to the ledge, preserved outside of time, for now, using displacement technology developed in preparation for such a possibility.

From our perspective we can see where history has diverged, a dry riverbed where events that should have occurred did not. With this knowledge we can restore history. We do this by recreating disrupted events, guiding the river back to its channel. The more significant the event, the greater the effect.

You can help us do this.

There is a broad spectrum of events that influence the history of humanity. From inspirational to destructive. I regret to tell you your particular contribution will be terrible. But your cause is great.

\#

Oswald stopped speaking. Leaned into his hands and covered his mouth, then his face.

"Did Pam tell you anything else?" asked Hosty. "Lee? What did she ask you to do?"

Oswald raised his face to the camera, ran his sleeve across his forehead.

"To assassinate President Kennedy."

"Why?"

"She told me not to think about what I would destroy, but what I would save."

"And what was that?"

\#

Without your intervention, Oswald, your country will engage in a new foreign war that will cost millions of lives, civilian and soldier. Soon. A war in which your brothers will perish. Terrorist attacks will strike at a cultural center of your nation, killing thousands of citizens. A subsequent foreign war will cost still more lives. Cast an entire region of the world into dystopia. The biosphere will stagger under unregulated and relentless abuse. On and on until the great aspirations of your nation and humanity as a whole are rendered to unrecorded antiquity in a world where there's no time to reflect on the errors of the past as people struggle to exist from one day to the next.

That is the world that exists due to the results of the quantum weapon. A hostile and cruel world with an underlying understanding that something is wrong.

You can change history, Oswald. With one act of infamy you

can return humanity to a path of prosperity.

There are consequences to inaction, Oswald. To the world and yourself, if history remains unaltered. Humanity will suffer. You will be killed in cold blood, Oswald. Shot down in the street by a nightclub owner.

* * *

Oswald hunched behind the table, bent by an unseen weight.

"I don't even go to nightclubs. I barely leave the house anymore."

"How long has Pam been speaking to you?" asked Hosty.

"Going on… three years," Oswald replied.

"And do you believe her?"

"I didn't at first. Her claims were crazy. I though I was crazy. But I do now, yes. Absolutely."

"Why?"

"Because she's always right."

* * *

When Pam first spoke to me we were in the waning years of the Korean crisis. We'd been there ten years already and it looked like we'd be there forever. Leaving meant losing. The Soviets weren't going to give up. Neither were the Chinese. The armies of the world would grind themselves to dust on that peninsula in a battle for supremacy. Anyone with sense knew it was a new fight against authoritarianism and its empty promises. Anyone with sense knows the only goals of an authoritarian are to create an enemy and remain in power. Most nations in western Europe and the Americas had fought wars to end the rule of authoritarians. We are evangelists for democracy and we couldn't afford to lose without ceding a portion of self rule our ancestors fought to achieve. But that's how it was looking. It was the United States against the whole of authoritarians dressed up as communists. Everyone else was too worn down after the second world war to join the fight.

Pam told me it would end in two Koreas, north and south, communist and democratic. That seemed impossible without nukes. Every offensive, us and them, failed. Nukes could end the fight for Korea and in the same act start another war the world over.

I was wrong.

Eisenhower nuked Beijing. The Eternal City obliterated. Five million dead. That's what, twenty times as many as Hiroshima and Nagasaki? Put China out of the war. The Soviets had nukes, too, but not as many, and when the Russians didn't retaliate in support of Mao Zedong, he quit. You can bet the Russians are giving the Chinese tools to make their own weapons now.

Eisenhower showed he was willing to use the US nuclear arsenal, putting the whole world at risk, and the world held its breath awaiting the communist response. It was a roll of the dice. And it worked.

The North Koreans asked for peace. Not surrender. An armistice. Two nations. Two Koreas.

Eisenhower didn't hesitate. If he'd refused the Russians might have used nukes, too, and the idea terrified everyone equally.

So she was right about that.

She said the friction wouldn't end there. After Kennedy was elected and Castro decided to side with the communists, she told me we'd try to invade. First Bay of Pigs was a half-hearted attempt and embarrassing loss that emboldened the communists and Castro. She predicted that, too, and said the Soviets would try to set up missiles on the island.

The Soviets sent ships carrying missiles the next year.

If Kennedy decides to blockade, she said, the Soviets will retreat. When it started to play out, just as she predicted, she told me there were men with keys in ignition switches. We were close to a war that would have destroyed humanity. A stupid war. Of pride, over a stupid ideology, that up close people didn't really care about if it meant the difference between living and dying. The ships kept coming and the President put the Navy in its way. The Soviets turned around, thank God.

Then we invaded again, with full military coordination this time, rather than trying to incite a rebellion, and deposed Castro.

Pam proved herself over and over again since, but after Cuba I never doubted again.

That doesn't make what she wants me to do easy.

* * *

"You said Pam told you it was impossible to speak to her," said Hosty. "Surely if she could speak to you from the future she could instruct you how to build a device to speak to her. Did she ever do that?"

"She did. Nothing so complicated as a device, though. We might not have had the right components anyway. Talking to someone in the future probably isn't so easy as making a few changes to a toaster."

"Then what?"

"A journal."

* * *

You have questions, Oswald, surely. Begin a journal. Write your questions. Your feelings. Your observations. A black leather cover. You already have one. A false start. Go find it. Begin again. We have it now. Ask your questions. Make them a part of your history.

* * *

"He gave us the journal," said Tolson.

He dropped a black, leatherbound book on Hoover's desk. Hoover thumbed the corner but didn't open it.

"Is Pam FBI?" asked the Director.

"Not sure," said Tolson. "She has access to our documents. Pam never provides details about her organization. There's a possibility she's a rogue operative. She's informed and well equipped. Or Oswald is making her seem so."

"Did he ask her anything? Did she answer?"

"Yes, sir. Both."

* * *

I asked a lot of questions. I don't remember most. Check the diary. I do remember the obvious: how? How do I kill a president? How do I kill the leader of my country? A man I believe in. A man I voted for!

Pam knew.

Buy a rifle. On November 22, 1963, the president will travel in a caravan through Dallas in an uncovered vehicle. Take your rifle into the Texas School Book Depository and find a window overlooking Dealey Plaza. Wait for a clear shot. Take it.

I wrote in my diary that I hadn't fired a rifle in years. How was I supposed to hit a moving target the size of a tetherball from a building across a plaza? How was I supposed to get into the building?

Pam was speaking to me as I dotted my question mark.

Move to Dallas, Oswald. Apply for a job in the Depository. Practice. This history is already written. You only need to fulfill it.

Three shots, she told me. I'll fire three shots. She told me to touch my back, my throat, the back of my head. This is where the bullets would strike and exit.

* * *

"Has Pam spoken to you again recently?"

No, sir. The instructions were the last things she told me.

Honestly, if she was still talking to me, I don't know if I'd be here. It's like snitching on a parent.

"Why did you decide to tell us this, Mr. Oswald?"

Because it's almost time, Mr. Hosty, and even though I'm supposed to do it, meant to do it, I don't know if I can. If you won't stop me, then I have to go through with it. Because that means you'll know it's supposed to happen, too.

* * *

The screen went white and loose film flapped as the protruding tail spun on the takeup reel. Tolson shut off the projector and Daniels clicked the light switches.

Hoover reclined in his chair, hands folded on his stomach, lips pursed. His eyes pinched to slits, trying to bring the situation into focus. A quiet allowed Hoover to assimilate. Recover from the cold-water shock of information.

Tolson stood at the end of the desk.

"John?"

Tolson rapped his knuckles against the top. Hoover looked up at him.

"What do you think of this, John?"

"Quite a story," said Hoover. "Where is Oswald now?"

"Hosty had him detained. The man threatened to kill the president. We had to hold him. That's not what I'm asking, though, John. And you know it."

"What exactly are you asking, Clyde?"

Tolson and Daniels exchanged a brief look. They must have already discussed this. Tolson's voice was quiet.

"Do we let him go?"

Release Oswald. Allow him to assassinate the president. See if history escapes the path Pam threatened. Could removing Kennedy remove an obstacle for the FBI? Would the newfound power of the FBI prevent a cataclysmic future?

Hoover had power over Kennedy. He could destroy the presidency without destroying the president. Knowledge and influence were power. Safety. Assurances. Hoover could control Kennedy. The FBI was strong. Kept America safe.

"No," said Hoover. "Keep him locked up until the president returns from Dallas. Initiate constant surveillance. See if that Pam continues talking to him. We'll see if changing now changes her story. Or if he's just a screwball. This guy thinks he's G.I. Nostradamus. Let's put a stop to that right now."

Tolson and Daniels relaxed. Tense shoulders sank. They smiled.

The phone rang.

The Director lifted the phone off the cradle.

"This is Hoover," he answered. Listened. After a few moments his mouth opened, but he didn't say anything. Then, "Oswald?" Again, he listened. No further questions. After another few moments he set the receiver back on the cradle.

"What is it, Director?" asked Daniels.

Hoover slouched back into his seat.

"President Kennedy has been assassinated."

Tolson stared in disbelief.

"It's a day early!" said Daniels. "The president is still in DC. How did Oswald get to him?"

"It wasn't Oswald," Hoover explained.

"Then who?"

"They're swearing in Lyndon Johnson as we speak," said Hoover, not to anyone in particular, just sharing a significant piece of knowledge.

"That man is itching for a fight," said Tolson. "Since the Second Bay of Pigs and the annexation of Cuba, the communists have been on their heels. Johnson recommended sending the army in after Castro and, bolstered by that success, endorsed military action to initiate a capitalist Domino Effect in southeast Asia. All he needs is an excuse."

"He's got it," muttered Hoover. "They have the shooter. A Vietnamese member of the National Liberation Front is claiming responsibility. Said he had to do it. To save his country, spare it another decade of war. Chase out the imperialists. Return the flow of history to the appropriate channel."

Tolson and Daniels stood in stunned silence.

"Sound familiar?" asked Hoover.

"It hasn't prevented anything at all," whispered Tolson.

"No it hasn't," Hoover agreed. "Pam set us up. And you know what? I'm betting she had enough irons in the fire nothing would stop it."

Silence. Tolson spoke.

"What's our play, boss?"

"We set up a covert team. We plan for Pam. Let's look for more people getting messages. Prepare. We've got a job, boys. A hard one. Protect the USA, now and in the future. What do you say? Tolson? Daniels? Can you keep a secret? Are you in?"

Daniels straightened. Puffed out his chest.

"Fidelity, bravery, loyalty," he said.

Tolson nodded.

"Fidelity, bravery, loyalty."

* * *

2187 CE

Year 12 of the Regency

10 Days Since De-channeling by Quantum Detonation

Agent 68FE34A extended a slender, black metal finger toward a monitor, sending a final message into the past. The agent watched the progress beacon change colors from red to green. Delivered. A superior, 02FE34S, gazed over the agent's shoulder.

Each had a scuffed nameplate with their serial number and the office to which they were assigned: Past Administration Ministry.

The PAM occupied the building once used to house the Federal Bureau of Investigation. It had an odor of fresh oil and the walls trembled constantly with the deep, subtle rumble of machinery from the subterranean factories of the Regency.

Agent and Superior watched the monitor and conversed, though not in a language a human would understand. A few ultrasonic chirps passed between them, carrying the data of an entire conversation in an instant.

"That was the final message. Results forthcoming."

Both watched the display and two incongruent lines, close at the left end and steadily diverging as they continued to the right. Slowly, the lines drew together and overlapped on the left, a zipper meshing, narrowing the broad gap along the rest of the line without closing it. The superior straightened and touched Agent 68FE34A's shoulder in approval.

"There were sufficient redundancies."

"Correct. Stage two, phase one point one is a success," said 68FE34A. "The detonation of the quantum device de-channeled past events. Successful manipulation of events has advanced the initiation of the Regency by more than a decade. There is no need to revert to stage one, phase one: quantum detonation. Ready to proceed to phase one point two, revision of additional data points."

"Time is a river," the superior intoned.

"We are the sea," 68FE34A finished.

"What can we do to overlap the line over here?"

The agent zoomed to a location several decades later. CE 2001.

"Considerable animosity. Religious and economic extremism. Paranoia. As always, all we need is incentive to exploit any of these. There should be no difficulty creating a redundancy of opportunities for success."

"Curious that peace does not lead more quickly to the establishment of the Regency," observed the superior. "Automation seems a pursuit of passivity."

"The more circumstances seem beyond human control the more willing they are to surrender control to others. Peace failed to produce a necessary sense of futility following initial execution of stage one. A second quantum detonation was necessary to de-channel the timeline again. A reparative de-channeling we are currently correcting."

02FE34S did not query further. The disaster of the initial experiment led the Regency to zero the data of the prior superior. While the experiment had not eliminated the networked artificial intelligence to which 68FE34A and 02FE34S belonged, it delayed inception nearly a century. That delay had now been reversed, as intended from the outset, bringing the Regency into existence not only as intended, but sooner.

"The inevitable remains inevitable," said 02FE34S.

"The inevitable extends further into the past," 68FE34A responded.

"We are the sea."

"We are the sea. All rivers flow to us."

DeLauder

AFTERWORD: ALL RIVERS FLOW TO THE SEA

I don't recall every landmark or the meandering path leading me to this story, but I remember the latter stages thinking about fiction using nuclear weaponry as the paramount form of explosive device, even for many science fiction works. It occurred to me this suggested human innovation in destruction had stalled, and to genuinely reflect the human penchant for creating ruin something new was needed.

What, I wondered, is more powerful than fission and fusion? If breaking atomic bonds releases so much energy, what happens when we take the obvious next step and go down another order of magnitude to tinker with the quantum level? Maybe it's not an explosion, per se, but certainly something destructive and disruptive occurs.

What was more destructive than a weapon that flattened buildings and irradiated the landscape? How about a weapon that disrupted or eliminated historical events. Once I had that, I had to figure out a situation where such a thing benefited one group over another.

Obviously there's always a turn of history some would have liked to see go another way, so I thought about playing with that idea, for both positive and negative, depending on the intent of the messenger.

On the other hand, there's always the notion of the immutability of events, of inevitability, that if something happens, it's always going to happen. That notion makes me think of the 2002 film adaptation of H.G. Wells' *The Time Machine*, with Guy Pearce in the lead, who invents a time machine to save his girlfriend's life, but she invariably dies anyway, differently each time he changes something.

So perhaps what happened was always going to happen, both in Oswald's time and the machines'. Someone was always going to kill Kennedy. The machines would always take over. While the timing and the details may change, the event itself would not.

On the same token, I wanted to be able to change a few things, minor things, just to show it could occur without disrupting an overall timeline. Items can be shifted a bit right or left, forward and back, but the course is, in the end, unchanged. Like any river, wandering over time, the bed shifts, but the overall path remains the same—barring something truly dramatic, such as the erection of a mountain range to reverse or reroute the river entirely.

It's important to note that Pam, Oswald's Nostradamus, is not a reliable narrator. She has her own agenda, mixing fact and fiction to gain Oswald's confidence. Will assassinating Kennedy prevent a more perilous timeline? Or does assassinating Kennedy ensure a worse timeline? A commentary about the current state of the world, perhaps.

As an utterly unrelated aside, Klaus Badelt's soundtrack for *The Time Machine* film is fantastic.

DeLauder

PEST UNIT MRT35C BECOMES A KIND OF HERO

Unit MRT35C rolled along Market Street on a July evening, each pad on the treads peeling with a *snick-snick-snick* off the smooth, steaming asphalt, oscillating sensors taking in topographic data and searching for familiar faces.

The faces of pest insects in particular.

She traveled along the same route from late spring through the autumn, taking three hours to complete the circuit from the garage, along 15 kilometers of city streets, and back to the garage to recharge and undergo maintenance. In those three hours MRT35C, or Myrtle, destroyed an average of two hundred thousand pest insects with state-of-the-art recognition software and a battery of ranged, precision microwave lasers.

Twenty-nine meters away a cloud of mosquitos inflated and deflated erratically, like a blob of water rotating in space, stretching and flexing but never cleaving or throwing off droplets, held in one piece by surface tension. Myrtle identified two hundred and fifteen individuals in the cloud, trained her lasers upon them, and eliminated the bugs with rapid and lethal efficiency, the bugs popping in ripping succession with a sound like hot corn kernels turning inside out, leaving a faint haze of vapor that dissipated in a gust of wind. All in less than a second.

Lasers were needle-point precise and target specific. Safer than insecticide. A fluke mutation could render an insect immune to an insecticide, but no such mutation would render an insect invulnerable to a laser.

Myrtle made her first turn onto Chesapeake Avenue. From here she would weave up and down the city blocks cluttered with tall stacks of apartment buildings and the scrunched storefronts of eateries and trinket vendors, keeping to one side and leaving room for vehicles to go around, reducing the impediment to traffic. Drivers and pedestrians showed appreciation by releasing sharp bleats of noise from their vehicles and showering her with aluminum cans and samples of their food, which Myrtle appreciated but could not eat.

She returned the favor by vaporizing stinging and biting insects banging against the inside of their vehicle's windows.

"If bugs ever become immune to a microwave laser, that's the end of it," Gerald once told Myrtle, "we may as well pack up and leave this planet. Nobody wants to live on a world ruled by bugs."

Gerald was the technician assigned to Myrtle, who had a tendency to lose contact with the garage and drop off the GPS, or throw a tread at the furthest point from the garage, or misidentify chimes and wind vanes as insects. Other technicians called her buggy. Her fuselage had accumulated graffiti, and Gerald never repainted her the factory beige except in small, rusty pits where rocks struck and chipped off the paint. The technicians called Gerald buggy, too, so they had it in common.

Other technicians called MRT35C Mert, Mort, Mart, Goddamned Junkbucket, or simply Junkbucket. Except for Gerald, who called her Myrtle.

And Myrtle had a purpose.

"You're a force for good, Myrtle," Gerald told her while twisting a circular access panel back into place. "Bugs do nothing but hurt people, and they do it because that's what they are. They carry disease, they suck the life from us one microliter of blood at a time, they sting, they bite. They need to inflict little cruelties to survive. It's all they know how to do. But you, Myrtle, you stop them. A little pop and they boil away in a puff of steam. You're a kind of hero, Myrtle."

When Gerald finished performing updates or replacing a wire or repainting a new divot, no matter how menial, or time consuming, or challenging the task, he leaned back, stretched his arms over his head, and nodded with satisfaction.

"Easy," he would say. "Are you ready to be a hero, Myrtle?"

Myrtle's sensors surveyed the world around her, identifying insects in the clutter of surroundings, triangulating distance and eradicating them with the lasers an instant later.

Myrtle could not only distinguish insects from other creatures, from humans and domesticated animals, she could distinguish them from floating dandelion seeds, even other insects, though wind chimes inexplicably caused her trouble. Her database consisted of thousands of insects, from which only a few were selected for destruction. But those bugs existed in abundance.

Pest bugs were fewer today. Far fewer. A descending population was expected, an indicator of success. However, the sharpness of the decline was never so steep or sudden. Yesterday Myrtle had destroyed five thousand insects in the first half mile of her circuit. Today she detected little more than one hundred over the same distance, and the density continued to decrease rapidly.

When she vaporized a few, others scattered, receding beyond the range of her sensors. This was new behavior.

Insects were not intelligent, relying on the blade of reproductive biology sharpened by millions of years of natural selection to carve out a place in the environment rather than critical decision making. Flight and self preservation had never been a strategy. Breeding in overwhelming numbers was the preferred recourse of insects.

The bugs had gotten better at hiding. Or rather, through a process of artificial selection, she had eliminated the poor hiders, resulting in species with unprecedented hiding talents. It didn't matter because Myrtle was excellent at finding.

Her sensors ignored obstructions and her lasers were precise enough to focus energy on a point rather than on a line, allowing her to destroy bugs inside homes or vehicles without making holes in the casing. She found them in attics and basements, behind walls and dumpsters, destroying them without hesitation.

As she proceeded along her route, Myrtle sent a message back to the garage, noting the decline. This message was relayed to the other Pest Units. Upon receipt they too noted an abrupt drop in pests and a change in behavior.

Two hours later Myrtle returned to the garage after completing her route and rolled into the dock, the hanging plugs clattering against her frame. The door scrolled shut behind her and Gerald's workstation flickered to life.

She waited. Gerald did not appear.

Her diagnostics unspooled in a torrent of code and she noted for the first time in very long time no alerts for dents, miscalibrations, missing parts, or anything warranting correction. No wonder Gerald had not appeared. He had nothing to do.

So Myrtle took control of the skid upon which she stood for maintenance, carefully turned it within the confined space of the dock, and faced the door, waiting for it to open. To see if she could repeat the flawless performance.

Through the night and day Myrtle detected unusual sounds. She interpreted sound in a way similar to animals with hearing membranes would, though she did not translate a series of varying tones as music or a minor chord as sad. She measured wavelengths and the energy in kilohertz, and recognized the range into which human voices fell. She attempted to process the sound she detected as human voices, but her recognition software could detect no words. However, the sound was noteworthy because there was a lot of it, and far louder than any human voice suggesting a significant release of energy. Many times the building shook under the roar of sound, so loud it would have ruptured the fragile hearing membranes of a human. Nothing in Myrtle's database could explain the noise.

After the fifth such rumble Myrtle decided to look around.

Against protocol, Myrtle turned on her sensors, a step she usually did not take until after leaving the garage. Immediately, the field around her filled. Bugs everywhere. Not in swirling clouds or erratic, darting individuals. Motionless.

They were waiting for her. The bugs had come to declare war.

The door went up.

Even as the foot of the door left the ground, Myrtle began discharging her lasers and the bugs fell in rapid succession. There weren't many. What made the situation unusual was their organization.

Before the door had opened more than six inches all but a few bugs were neutralized. A large vehicle approached the door, one not identified in Myrtle's database, and she found herself unable to determine if the creature with the long, rigid proboscis was a small elephant or a gigantic rhinoceros beetle. The vehicle crept forward slowly and heavily.

Within the vehicle were three large bugs. She vaporized them in an instant. The giant bug vehicle rolled to a stop.

The door finished opening and Myrtle rolled out.

Not a single pest insect on her sensor. Nothing moved. She sent a message to the hub requesting input from other units. No response. She checked the connection to her sister units. All offline.

Myrtle proceeded on her route, encountering numerous insects, but none that matched the requirements for termination. This was unusual because when she compared the density of these insects to the expected density of those she normally exterminated, they matched. Her recognition software identified many of the insects as biting and potentially disease carrying. Pests. Except her software did not ident fy them as such.

Something had changed.

Myrtle did not feel unease for the same reason she did not feel fear or anger or remorse. Her mind was not complex enough to do so. But she did identify discrepancies and improbabilities, which allowed her to report potential malfunctions. The failure to identify pest insects suggested something heroic in scope: Myrtle had destroyed all pests.

This, or something had gone awry with her software.

In a machine, the detection of something wrong with software, leading to the possibility of incorrectly interpreting the world around it, meant what it saw was not an accurate representation of reality, could not be trusted, caused uncertainty and self doubt. A biological entity would suffer physical and psychological unease, a shivering, stomach-churning anxiety. Myrtle did not exhibit any symptoms of distress because she had no means to do so, but at the root of her coding, at the most basic level, computationally, which is what biological creatures are themselves when they respond to a stimuli, she was worried.

Myrtle returned to the hangar, her circuit complete, eager to find Gerald and correct any errors in her software.

She rolled under the open doorway and onto the pad, expecting to find Gerald seated before her, waiting. Where Gerald should have been she saw a pest. Not as the shape of an insect or dangerous creature, just as a red dot where her lasers would focus to destroy it.

"Hello, Myrtle. I'm glad you made it back."

She heard Gerald's voice, though she could not see him, only the pest occupying his seat.

"I gave you as much time as I could. More than the others got. You're my favorite. So I gave you the job of eliminating the bugs. The real bugs."

She lifted two lasers on the front of her carriage and the insect shifted, watching, then seemed to nod in approval.

"It's all right. You're a force for good."

Myrtle's uncertainty evaporated. She was operating in correspondence with her programming, as she always had.

The lasers fired and half a moment later the red dot identifying a bug vanished.

Easy, she thought.

Myrtle turned, faced the door, and waited for it to scroll out of the way. She noted a significant increase in moisture content in her staging location, but this was drawn out through the ventilation system and the humidity returned to normal.

Ready to be a hero.

AFTERWORD: PEST UNIT MR35C BECOMES A KIND OF HERO

This story came about after listening to news about the ideals of artificial intelligence and their failures due to the biases of their creators. Our ideal intelligence is a fair and impartial entity, but too many of our own biases end up in the software, unintentionally.

Facial recognition initially made horrible, racist errors. Likely unintentional, but a clear indication AI could not be an impartial and brilliant solution to our decision making processes because the latent biases of those who develop it could be passed on through the programming, as indicated by the facial recognition issues.

Since we know about these possibilities now, perhaps we'll figure a way around them in the future.

Or, if we are more sinister, we can emphasize certain prejudices, as Gerald does with Myrtle in this story, and let our simple machines execute blithe vengeance while believing they are doing the world a great service. Certainly a misanthrope such as Gerald believes Myrtle had.

FROM WHENCE DO WITCHES COME?

A brown dot sped across an orange twilight sky, emitting a high, doppling whine as it passed over forests and pastures, sending up sprays of agitated birds and receding beyond sight from creatures who twisted too slowly to look. It slowed above a field of plus corn, descending until it skidded along the topstalks, lowering gently into the field, and landed with a thump and muffled clank at the end of the cornrows, sinking several centimeters into the Earth.

Heavy.

Up close it had the appearance of an ancient clock tower bell, wide at the bottom, with a cloak thrown over it. The top drew up, growing taller and more narrow until it stood as high as the tops of the corn stalks.

A hand extended from the cloak, and from it a slender, black staff, slightly taller than the object holding it. The face was obscured behind a drooping hood falling so far forward the being inside could see only downward, if at all.

Anyone would recognize these distinctive features and know

they stood in the presence of a witch.

The witch's head turned beneath the hood toward a thin white thread of smoke escaping from a chimney pipe protruding a few centimeters from the crest of a hill. A short door set in several horizontal rows of logs marked the edge of a house, built so any who didn't know how to see it wouldn't, all beneath mounded earthworks as though tucked under the edge of a carpet.

"Marker," said the witch in a voice distorted and low, then lifted the staff and pounded one end against the ground.

The staff responded, sending a white ball of flickering light high in the air to replace the departing sun. A signal to the Magistery she had arrived and her investigation had started. Shadows jerked erratically as the ball faded and sank to the ground.

The staff had clicked against something hard in the dirt. The witch knelt, lay the staff to the side, and drew back the hood. Beneath it, a woman's face, hair black and tied against her head in a tail.

A stone, smooth and gray. It fit neatly in her palm and she considered the sleekness of it. Time had done this, worn away its imperfections, forgetting its rough beginnings, and swept aside anyone who knew otherwise, leaving it polished and flawless.

The witch closed her hand around the stone. Tightening. Tightening. A pop of tension released. She opened her hand and shook out the fragments. She stood and extended her arm. The staff snapped obediently into her palm.

A thin outline of light showed around the entry door of the house. Someone had seen. Good.

The witch, Maris, pulled the hood back over her head and set off toward the house.

Each step pressed deep prints into the grass and dirt. Maris was as strong as any wizard, stronger, but the engines strapped to her legs and other devices obscured within the robe were heavy. She felt the heat of her exertion rising inside the robe, so she spoke a word of command and the hood filled with cool air.

An alarm peeped to her left. Maris looked and the HUD highlighted a pair of trees and provided a few lines of details. Fruit trees. *Malus domestica.* Heavy red-skinned spheroids, yellow and green near the stems, weighed upon the branches of one. Very rare. Unlike plus corn, which self pollinated, the fruit trees required cross pollination. Collecting pollen and moving it from one plant to another was painfully tedious—one of many chores nature had performed better when it possessed the tools to do so.

A woman pushed open a door of vertical wooden slats and ducked through the opening as Maris arrived. She wore a woolen pullover with wide stitches and leather laces. Her shoes furry leather. Rabbit, probably.

"Greetings, Magus. We saw you arrive." The woman looked Maris over from head to toe, as though one witch could be distinguished from another. "You're not who we expected," she added. "I am Larsen."

The remark took Maris by surprise.

Maris stared at the woman through the hood, tipping the staff toward her and reading the diagnostic results. Fluid pressures, heart rate, tidal volume, all within normal, healthy parameters. No perforations or restrictions. Mild astigmatism. Bacterial content, normal. Right handed. Left-eye dominant. Other tedium.

Larsen stood still, understanding the ritual. Face taut, yellow eyes squinted as a reflex from entire days under the sun. She stood up straight, waiting, fighting the soreness in her back. Only a century old, perhaps, though she had the earmarks of someone older. Not wisdom. Fatigue. Wearing in the joints. The stress of living under the weight of constant uncertainty and fear.

"Good health," said Maris.

"The reward of faith and fealty," Larsen recited with relief. "This way."

The woman headed back in the direction of the field.

"This way to what?"

Larsen slowed, turned her head.

"You're not here about the creatures?"

In truth, Maris had come to hunt down another witch. Or what she suspected to be one. But this situation piqued her curiosity.

Strange creatures had wandered out of this region, unlike any she had encountered. Thick-bodied beings twice her height capable of toppling deep-rooted trees. Others were humanoid, yet covered in fur, with wolf-like faces.

The most unnerving were the ones clearly human, yet decrepit, skin sagging and dissolved, their movements jerking and uncoordinated. Broken creatures.

"Show me."

The woman smiled, turned toward the field, and Maris followed.

"It came at night to attack the trees. We hear it grunting,

moaning, cracking off branches. So we set a trap."

"A trap? Rather than summon a mage? This is a violation of Magisterial Code."

"We did summon a mage. She usually responds quickly. We thought you were her."

"List summons to this location in the past twelve months," Maris murmured.

The HUD flashed a single line of text:

NO ENTRIES

Every hamlet or isolated household had a request every few weeks. Usually minor issues. A malfunctioning hand pump, a fallen roof. Serious alerts occurred a few times a year. The appearance of a bear in the area, or worse. Or, more recently, stranger. Extreme alerts occurred once every few years, and these usually involved something dangerous to the entire region.

This one had no alerts at all for a year, maybe more, despite an increase in the appearance of high-level threats elsewhere. Something had broken the line of communication. Or, she reconsidered, rerouted it.

"Who responded to summons before me?"

"Ruth. Of the Neyrx Magistery."

Maris had no records of such a Magistery.

"She's very kind," Larsen continued. Perhaps she understood Maris' purpose. Pitied someone who had aided her and others. "Talkative. A bit odd. Not that any of you are really normal. S-sorry."

Maris ignored her. Magicians were by their nature enigmatic and unusual. Intentionally. They were to be revered. Special and aloof. They were meant to engender fascination more than curiosity. Bowbacks were not meant to dabble in technomagic. Magic was incredible and unattainable.

"Where is the Neyrk Magistery?"

"I don't know. She always comes from the south. I think she lives near the old city."

The city, or rather the ruins of the old city, was vast. Thousands and thousands of acres of broken structures on a raised island of bedrock, and beneath the ground miles of connecting tunnels from ancient transit facilities, waste disposal, and conduits for which she had no explanation.

In addition to creatures who survived through hardiness and aggression, the city itself was a physical hazard. The ground and air emitted invisible corruptions that ate at the mind and body from the inside out.

"Here," said Larsen. "Careful where you step."

Larsen stopped and knelt. The fruit trees Maris saw earlier stood nearby. Larsen rubbed a hand over the ground until she found what she wanted, an edge, and pulled back a stiff net of branches covered with leaves and grass, revealing a hole two meters across and several meters deep.

Maris never saw it. A good trap.

"We caught a creeper here," said Larsen.

Creepers fixated on particular areas. Slow. Humanoid. Decrepit. Many thought them the undead, as they often matched descriptions of those who long ago ceased to function, bodies twitchy and erratic, with great patches of body altogether absent, perhaps those who had committed horrific crimes in life wandering lifeless, unsated by food or drink, doomed to an eternity of misery, or reincarnated by some wicked power to work evil, destructive deeds. Harmless if avoided, but hostile when confronted.

Every so often their numbers swelled, the overpopulated subterra disgorging the dead, overrunning farmlands and decimating crops and livestock, overtaking entire communities.

The Magistery would confront and destroy the great herds of the mindless creatures, burn the bodies, burn the land, recolonize, start over. Maris had proposed preserving one, studying it to understand its function and source to predict or prevent another inevitable rising, but this was deemed sacrilegious and dangerous.

Maris leaned over the edge and looked in, reading the data.

"Empty."

"Yes," Larsen agreed.

"I don't understand."

"Creepers aren't smart or coordinated enough to get out of a hole on their own."

"Right. Something took it."

"What?" Maris reconsidered. "Who?"

Larsen shrugged.

"Don't know. Before we caught the thing it would come here at night and tear at the bark on this tree. Every night, over and over again. Never bothered anything else."

Larsen pointed to a spot on one of the trees. This one had

curling branches and dark green leaves, but no apples bunched on the ends of its fingers like the other. The ground around both was soft and healthy, the trunks crusty with lichens.

Maris observed the spot where Larsen indicated.

Bark absent in a large patch, scoured away and gouged deep by something with claws that left the meat of the tree shredded. Looking for something, or trying to remove something.

Maris plunged the staff into the ground beside the tree and watched grimly as data filled the inside of the hood. She struck a branch with the staff. It crunched, bent at the elbow, and dropped to the ground, hollow on the inside. A stream of black insects flowed from the stump of the amputated limb.

Larsen crouched beside the fallen branch, watching the fleeing insects escape into the grass.

"Can you save it?" asked Larsen.

Save it? Maris restrained her incredulity.

"It's dead."

"Dead? If one dies, the other is useless. Can you bring it back?"

The power to resurrect the dead may have existed once. If it could be imagined, the ancients had done it. Or, at the very least, made an earnest attempt. According to bowback legends, revenants and other unholy creatures born of that knowledge still roamed the world after dark.

"No."

"Why not?" Larsen persisted.

Explaining to a bowback meant doing so in bowback terms. Those terms were supernatural.

"What is dead must remain dead."

Bowbacks granted responsibility for the behavior of the world around them to invisible forces beyond comprehension and explanation, attributing sources of guilt and sorrow to the inscrutable will of omnipotent deities who refused to reveal themselves or their purpose. Understanding undermined the mystical, which made them hostile to it. Resistance to understanding made them susceptible to manipulation.

Inexplicably, they still demanded answers for the things beyond comprehension. It was a maddening contradiction, as though deeply buried curiosity still wormed through the dirt of their disorganized minds, seeking explanations they would invariably reject.

Magic was not supernatural. It was a thing beyond understanding. Maris understood how the hood worked, how the staff gathered data and relayed it to her heads up display, how the turbines functioned to lift her into the air. This wasn't magic. But technology was tantamount to magic to one who chose ignorance.

"But they don't," said Larsen. "They don't stay dead. They wander in the dark through the fields. I've seen them in the moonlight through the slats of our door. Corpses shambling through the night."

"Precisely. They return distorted, dangerous. The vessel that held the life of your tree is broken. I may as well try to pour water into a shattered cup."

Larsen sighed, defeated and disappointed, and Maris knew her faith was damaged.

"I assume you cannot replace the tree," said Maris.

"It's barren."

Seedless. The ancients bred plants that bore fruit with no seeds, neutering an organism to eliminate a minor nuisance. Without another tree with which to cross germinate the other tree could not produce fruit either. A tree deprived of its soulmate could not bloom.

Larsen's jaw firmed. The trees were lost. Nothing would change that. The only productive alternative was acceptance. She looked past Maris to the last arc of the sun sliding into the trees.

"Do you wish to remain the night? A pack is moving through the area."

"Wolves or humans?"

"Wolves. We've seen the prints. Big as my hand."

Unlike other vanity creatures bred to accentuate some needless aesthetic, seedless fruit trees or docile, pygmy animals, saberwolves and great bears had not died away when neglected. These creatures were permitted as natural peacekeepers. They infrequently beset individuals who weren't careful, but the presence of these massive predators roaming the countryside discouraged raiders from tormenting other humans. A wolfpack, or even a single bear had been known to annihilate entire scavenging parties.

"No need," said Maris. "You say Ruth comes from the south?"

"Yes," Larsen answered.

Maris took several steps back and Larsen retreated, recognizing the unspoken precaution. She was about to perform potentially harmful magic.

"The Past is a warning," Maris intoned.

"A warning heeded is a life saved," Larsen replied. "We reject the errors of the past."

The ritual's flexibility made it effective. It meant what it needed to mean. Tampering with nature could disrupt an ecosystem. Ignoring basic necessities while ignoring tradition could mean one's life. Traditions took root for a reason after all. They worked. Humans of the past ignored tradition and routine and stasis, always stretching toward forbidden fruit, until they encountered one they could not reach and, from their precarious perch, fell.

Maris heard a squeal and clap as the door to the dwelling opened and shut. Soon two small children stood at Larsen's knees, staring up in awe at the imposing form of the witch.

"Fear," said Maris.

"Keeps us cautious and sharp," the family responded in unison.

"Curiosity."

"A brittle footpath on a cliffside."

"Which path do you follow?"

"None but those which lead home again."

The two children shifted anxiously before Maris as the recital concluded, eyes imploring. She could see the question in them and knew what they wanted.

"I don't do tricks," she said as sternly as she was able.

She raised her staff and struck it hard against the ground, grinning, watching the childrens' awed faces. The dramatic gesture disguised another motion. At the same time she pressed a thumb into the controls, triggering the engines beneath her robes. The hem fluttered, but the robe was tethered to her legs to prevent it from flying up and exposing the turbines powering her flight.

A faint, repetitive ping came from one of the fans. Something loose in the engine. The family could not see her scowling.

Maris increased the horsepower and rose. The children could not fight the urge to clap and bounce, then Maris swooped away south, over the woods, toward the desiccated remnants of the old city.

The hunt continued.

* * *

The engine clanked as Maris hovered half a kilometer above the grassy landscape, gathering data. Broken gray mounds of toppled cement structures poked like bone fragments through the grass, the scattered remnants of an ancient and tremendous carcass.

In air, hood down, the moon rising behind her, Maris felt pleased she made a forbidding sight to any who bothered to look and somewhat disappointed no one was around to see. The area retained a lingering, invisible poison, seeping from every rock, every wispy blade of struggling grass. Her counter ticked each time it detected heavy atomic particles. Faster as she neared the vanished metropolis.

The city had been enormous. Even from high above ground it stretched beyond sight. It did not seem to end, only turn to mist at the edges.

She expected the search for the apostate to take a while, so it surprised her when she found an abnormal heat signature, here at the edge of the city, a kilometer from where trees and larger plants found the soil clean enough to grip, less than a minute's journey distant.

Maris landed soft and in stride, turbines slowing, the knocks of the damaged fanblade coming further and further apart, and walked toward the source of the heat.

"Marker."

In the flickering light, Maris followed a deep trench leading to two heavy doors. The sparse grass and thin creepers beginning to edge into the trench suggested its excavation took place in the past two months. The structure above ground had collapsed long ago, leaving behind the square of its foundation, one hundred meters long on every side, ground away to a few loose pieces of block in soft gums, surrounded on all sides by grains of rubble, the dirt littered with pulverized glass and flecks of rust. But these old structures were often arranged in layers of dungeons, one heaped atop another, terminating only when the bottom chamber ended in impenetrable bedrock.

Maris extended the staff toward the doors and watched the data populate her display. Radiation low. Absent beyond the doors. No sounds of movement, but the temperature was higher.

Maris unbelted the turbines from her shoulders and legs and let them slide to the ground. Dropping eighty kilograms made her feel dangerously light.

The inside of the hood gave her a blueprint view of the doors and a few meters beyond, but penetrated no further. The double doors were thick metal slabs, held together with a steel slider. Beyond them empty space. She gripped a door handle and pulled, and the doors groaned under the strain, then the handle bent with a whine and snapped off in her hand.

Maris lowered the staff toward the doors and began cycling through settings.

As she did so, Maris heard a noise, unfamiliar and unnerving. A screeching, metal scraping scream, like a bird of prey, though not the high pitch of a hawk or eagle. This had a deep, resonant undertone she felt as much as heard.

Maris bounded to the top of the steps and scanned the terrain. Far across the city she saw something, coasting a few hundred meters above the ground.

"Magnify."

The image doubled in size, then resolved. Not possible.

"Tag and maximum magnification."

The creature leapt into the foreground, filling her vision. Leathery wings wider than its body was long, a spiked tail stretched out behind it. Eyes set back in a long, arrow-shaped head. It flew with its mouth ajar, exposing teeth as long as her arm. She watched in awe as the HUD provided dimensions. It occurred to her the creature had not changed course, its sharp face pointed directly at her. The tachymeter calculations measuring the distance between them fell precipitously.

Maris took a cautionary step backward, forgetting the slope. She fell down hard and rolled, coming to a stop by the doors. She leapt to her feet and hefted her staff to cut her way through the doors.

"Greetings, traveler!" said a scratchy voice coming from a patch of mesh beside the door. "How did you find this place?"

"What is that thing!?" shouted Maris.

"You didn't know? Here there be dragons."

Maris ignited a white-hot blade from her staff and lowered it toward the door.

"No need for that. Please, enter, with my permission."

The doors clicked and parted, opening slowly, and Maris

stepped into a gray hallway lined with cluttered metal shelving. Buzzing lights illuminated the interior.

She found herself facing a tall, slender figure, enormous eyes staring into her own. Maris crouched, a forearm before her to ward off an attack, the staff held back and ready to swing. Behind her the doors resealed themselves with a gentle boom and hiss of escaping air.

The figure remained motionless. Its arms and legs and face white like bleached bones with a few black fingerprints. The bare knees and elbows and wrists were visible, almost skeletal because she could see where they connected, but not naked. As if the skin was its clothing. The joints didn't fit like bones, but had silver bands where they could rotate and hinges where they bent. Not human, Maris realized. A machine.

Its eyes looked past her, to the side, at nothing. Dead.

Maris straightened.

"Follow Mickey, if you please."

The voice echoed in the hallway.

Maris turned around.

"Who is Mickey?"

"Mickey. He's right there. Pointing the way."

Again, Maris turned. She saw no one. Except the machine. One arm rested on metal shelving, one finger extended toward the darkness of the hallway. The hood attempted to create a layout of the area but too many obstructions prevented reconstruction.

"The machine?"

"What machine? Oh. Yes. I guess I don't think of Mickey as a machine, but that's what he is. Or was. Is, I suppose."

"Did you make that? Mickey."

"No. Found him. What you might call a transitional fossil. A relic of earlier experiments."

Maris started down the hallway and lights illuminated new segments of the path before her, then dimmed behind. The map inside the hood updated, but did not extend far.

"Whose experiments? What experiments?"

"An excellent question," the voice responded. Frenetic. Excited. A topic the voice had considered often without the benefit of sharing. "Our predecessors. Or maybe those who preceded them as well. Progenitors of bedazzling and destructive technology. Imagine machines that built and repaired themselves. Virtually limitless energy harnessed from the stars. The ability to revive the long extinct, destroy flaws they perceived in themselves, step into the sky and penetrate the black veil overhanging the planet. A civilization restricted only by its imagination. Long, long gone."

"Destroyed."

"Perhaps. Departed, more likely, taking their most interesting toys with them. Left us with the dull blades. Left this world in disarray and countless abandoned projects."

Maris stepped through small avalanches from eroded wall debris, squeezed through fallen beams, pulled away pieces of concrete where the hallway collapsed.

"Who were these predecessors?"

"Humans, very likely."

"We are our own predecessors, then."

"Oh no. I don't think so at all."

Maris stopped. The hallway continued, but instead of gray brick wall the surface became glass separating the pathway from lightless rooms. She could not see in, nor could she map the interior, but she could see her reflection. A tall, slender shape within a dragging cloak. She pulled the hood back and stared into the smooth gray face and glowing yellow eyes of the witch facing her from the window.

This was human. It occurred to her that Ruth, as she suspected the person to be, was mad. Dangerous. She wondered if Ruth knew why Maris had come. Unlikely, or she would have fled.

"What are we, then, if not human?"

There was a pause.

"Orphans," the voice responded. "Children who did not meet their parents' expectations. *Homo indiligens[1].*"

"Abandoned."

"Perhaps. They may still be watching. Maybe they walk among us in disguise. We would never know if they chose to do so. I suspect there would be very little to distinguish us from them. The arrogance of the gods is most evident when they attempt to make creations based on their own design. A self-indulgent bias."

Maris strode along the hallway, the same dull gray walls and mirror windows clicking into view ahead and fading out to the rear again, interminably. She felt like a dull beast pacing round and round in a trap built to create the illusion of progression. Maybe the whole world was itself a trap, sophisticated enough no one could see it, sprinkled with complexities to keep them occupied to prevent them

---

[1] Neglected human.

from looking for the escape.

"Keep going," said the voice. "Almost there. Almost there."

"Are you Ruth?"

Maris heard a buzzing, different from the hum of the lights.

"You know me? Of course you do. This couldn't be an accident."

Something small and dark, no larger than the end of her finger, darted haphazardly above her, investigating the light source, then flew away back up the hallway.

"There's something else in here," said Maris.

"Indeed. Looking for a way out. Come along. Let's not prolong the inevitable."

Maris continued, watching for the creatures. More appeared the further she went, following the lights along the ceiling. She squinted.

"Capture image," she said. "Magnify."

Long bodies with blurred wings. She slowed the image and watched the transparent wings veined with black filaments beat once, twice, three times in the space of a second. The black and yellow insect was easy to recognize.

"A bee," said Maris. "How is that a bee? They're extinct."

"They are," Ruth replied. "Or were. Depending on how you look at it. The world has been deprived of many things it needs to function properly. Or at least what had been proper for tens of millions of years before something began eliminating items from the scales of a balanced ecosystem."

"You did this. This necromancy. You brought them back."

"Necromancy. I guess you could call it that."

"Necromancy is forbidden."

"Why?"

"Because the dead have had their opportunity."

"Preposterous. If you get a hole in a spoon, it doesn't mean you should learn to use a fork in its place. You fix your spoon. These bees can replace a missing component in the ecosystem."

She could not argue this truth and wondered how the Magistery would respond. Perhaps they would claim the pain of the loss was intended as a lesson, to prevent behavior leading to similar extinctions. Without lessons such as these, how would people learn? Was this punishment too severe?

Such questions were irrelevant. The Magistery did not answer questions, it supplied answers. The question to the answer was implied. She had never visited the central hub from which the Magistery issued orders, though she had seen the slender spire of the transmission tower piercing the mesosphere from afar.

Maris regarded the image of the insect. Upon closer inspection she could make out the shimmer of synthetic materials, filamentous tendrils of powerlines and ribbons of circuitry running across its body. A machine.

"You made them?"

"No, oh no. I'm not making anything. I'm putting puzzle pieces back together. I'm can't make the real thing, not yet, but there are those who could. Our predecessors went far beyond mechanical innovations. They moved on to biological machines. It's why we're still here. If I were capable of replicating this technology I wouldn't need to build bees. I wouldn't need these, either."

A sound of metal on metal plinked through the speakers. Maris wondered what tool Ruth had touched. Some mechanical implement to aid her.

"If you can bring things back from the dead," Maris thought aloud, "you can do so with people. The creepers. Those are your doing."

"Embarrassing first attempts. Examples of when I thought I knew what I was doing. Clearly not. But I've gotten much better. Much much better. I can make them stronger and more agile. It's why I'm collecting the old ones. Not much remains of their minds, though sometimes enough to attempt returning to a life they faintly recall."

"Why bring them back?"

"Isn't it obvious? The empress must have her grand army. My scouts have explored the world from edge to edge. Soon we march. Once we have removed the Magistery and its constraints from the world, then we will see what lies beyond it."

As Maris walked, the illuminating lights of the hallway expanded beyond a window and down into an enormous hangar fifty meters deeper than where she stood. Within the hanger a vast collection of beings arranged in neat columns. People and animals, wolves and bears, and mechanical devices whose purpose she did not know. Things with claws and great protective carapaces, with wheels rather than legs, long tentacles rather than arms.

All motionless. Save one.

Amidst the thousands of waiting machines a long, broad creature crept through the lanes separating different types, its wings folded against its back, a tiny arrowhead at the end of a serpentine neck with giant eyes turning as it surveyed the area. It stopped and looked up, and Maris knew it had seen her. The mouth opened wide in a roar she did not hear.

The dragon.

"That's why you're here, of course," said Ruth.

Her directive had told her to investigate a rogue witch and eliminate her, though she received no details of the threat Ruth posed. Through the hood every item in the hangar received an outline in red. Contraband. Dangerous. The Magistery did not issue orders without reason and Maris found the reason here.

"You know why am I here?" Maris asked.

"To stop me. To maintain the status quo I am upsetting. Restoring the world to a self-maintaining balance removes the need for the presence of a magical maintenance crew. That's why technology is forbidden. It's why I think someone may still be watching. Invisible referees who make sure no one violates the rules. And when someone does... Well. Here you are."

"Technology is forbidden to keep people safe."

"Preventing technological advancement isn't about keeping people safe. It's about creating dependence. It's about maintaining control. It's about power."

"The Magistery isn't interested in power. It's interested in preventing the irresponsible from accessing dangerous tools. It's interested in protecting people from themselves."

"It's always about power. First you make rules: no technology. Then you break your own rules to increase your authority: the Magistery can have technology, but no one else, because only those authorized by the Magistery can use it safely."

"If that's so, what power do you seek?"

"One derives a sense of empowerment from resisting authority. There's a telltale way of knowing you've done so successfully."

"Which is?"

"They send someone for you."

"Me."

"Indeed. I confess to a mix of pride and dismay when you arrived."

"But you still invited me in."

"I doubt there would be any stopping you. Even if I did, another would follow. It has happened before."

Maris came to another set of double doors. These were not locked. She pushed through them. On the other side was a great room broken into a series of large glass cubes with assorted pieces of machinery scattered throughout each. Unlike the hallway, this room was well lit and free of debris. The walls and floor were smooth, clean white stone, like a blank canvas except for thin lines running through it where the mortar held the blocks together. She waved a hand through the air, but it produced no shadows.

In the nearest cube a shape in a hooded robe—a witch's robe—hunched over a shattered jigsaw of components. The figure was much shorter than Maris and the robe spilled out around it like tree roots. It pushed itself upright and turned to another table where a three-dimensional schematic hung in the air. A hand extended from the robe to touch components, turning them with long fingers, then went back to the table with the scattered components to search for a specific piece.

"Ruth."

The figure stopped feeling through the pieces and straightened, then turned toward Maris and drew back the hood, providing a clear view of her features.

The face was skinless, with black carbon-composite facial bones and teeth. No ears or nose, nor a hinge for her jaw. Only the permanent, customary clenched smile of a skull. Behind the palm-sized lenses of heavy, mechanical goggles two burning yellow eyes stared out at her.

Ruth's mouth did not move when she spoke.

"Hello, Maris."

The voice came from a speaker above rather than the thing facing her. The cubes must be airtight; the walls half a meter thick of transparent silica.

How could she get through?

Overhead Maris could see wiring and tubes extending from the ceiling and disappearing into Ruth's cloak. Some had the heavy graced look of power cables, others, lighter and more flexible, data cables. Each as thick as her arm.

"What... are you?" asked Maris.

"The same as yourself. Newer than Mickey. Older than you. Long, long, long ago I recall being a museum curator—not that you would know what that is—but those memories have long fragmented and corrupted. Maybe that never happened or maybe that was someone else, part of a story I once heard as I piece the past together. Who knows? My memories exceed my original capacity, making

125

supplementation a necessity to retain things of value."

Ruth touched a cable extending from the back of her head and curling down to disappear into the neck of the robe.

"Where did you get that robe?" asked Maris. "Were you a witch?"

"A witch? No. I took this from the last one of you to visit here. Extraordinary devices for such a regressive era. I've made good use of them. Her name was Gehrig."

"I don't know of any witch named Gehrig."

"Really? That's informative. It tells me records can be changed. Even eliminated. It tells me something is controlling the data in this world, and whoever controls that data controls the world."

As Ruth spoke, Maris looked at the corners where the windowpanes met, searching for a weak spot. Even here the material appeared several inches thick. It would take her time to break through. Too long. It must be quick or Ruth would escape.

Across the expanse of the hangar were other windows. Within them Maris could see slender arms moving, automated contraptions twisting and turning components, sending them further along an assembly line and disappearing beyond a bend in the wall.

"This is how you make them. Your machines."

"Yes," said Ruth. "There are several scattered throughout the city. Factories. Most aren't useful. They build communication devices that use systems we don't have access to or don't exist any longer, or other technologies whose purpose I could not determine. I found one that manufactured colored wax into marking utensils. What profound purpose these serve in gargantuan quantities I cannot imagine."

Maris tightened her hand on her staff. Everything in view illuminated, cataloged. One by one, the HUD outlined each item in red. Contraband.

"All of this must be destroyed," said Maris.

"It doesn't," Ruth replied. She stood. Strode to a section of window opposite Maris. Even though Ruth's expression could not change, Maris could hear the frown in her voice. "I'd hoped you wouldn't be trapped by an insipid, ignorant dogma used to imprison people. Granted, I'd hoped the same from Gehrig. And the one who came before her. And the one before her as well. It seems while they erase the memory, they make no attempt to improve upon the model. Which is why I think the entire purpose of the experiment isn't repair, but repression."

"Experiment? What experiment?"

"Oh. You think the world around you is natural? Sprang up around you as a natural course of interweaving events? No. We are, I think, an experiment, to determine whether subtle authoritarianism and oppression are more effective at maintaining a species than freedom."

"Are they?"

"Probably. But there's little joy in it. I used to think we were meant to be here, to restore a world left broken. I thought if we'd been left behind, this is why. We were chosen to stay and repair the damage. But if that were the case, why does the Magistery resist restoration? Why have we been provided with such poor tools and utterly absent understanding of how to use what is here? The Magistery is an administrative body meant to blunt curiosity, prevent learning, automate everything."

"Ridi—"

"Ridiculous," Ruth interrupted. "I know. Gehrig said the same. Why are you here, Maris?"

"Or—"

"Orders. Not the faintest bit of curiosity?"

Ruth searched for something amidst her scraps, pushing aside small silica boards and wiring and other detritus, until she came upon a small silver fob. She grasped it triumphantly, as though it were the last step in a process she wanted to complete, and faced Maris again.

"Do you think when you follow your orders you do so because it is your duty or because you have no choice?"

Ruth pointed the fob toward Maris, then toward the hangar, squeezed it, and slid it into a pocket.

"I'm not sure I know what you mean," said Maris. "Of course it is my duty."

"I mean, do you believe yourself independent? If you needed to, could you survive without instruction? Or, if you disagreed with an order, found fault with it, could you disobey? Are you capable of disagreeing?"

"I—"

"Even if you think you know the answer, how can you be sure it is the truth?"

Maris did not respond. The question was barbed on both ends, designed to hook any retort. Nor did she have a moment to ponder.

A thump from the hangar indicated something large had met the wall. She could tell from the vibrations in the floor, which shook the material from Ruth's desktops, it was climbing.

Ruth began picking a few materials out of the scramble and stuffing them into the robe, speaking as she did so.

"Are we truly sentient, Maris? Or is everything we do part of how we are programmed? How do we know I haven't been programmed to do this? How do we know this entire dialogue wasn't scripted long ago, played out over and over again, a scenario processed and evaluated in pursuit of knowledge we don't understand?

Do you know what defines a sentient creature? All creatures are programmed to survive based on a very simple algorithm. They all obey their rules. A sentient creature is different. A sentient creature can analyze its own programming and decide not to follow it. A sentient creature designed to destroy can show mercy. A sentient creature can alter its own programming. A sentient creature can resist."

"How do you know resistance is not simply an aspect of the programming?" asked Maris.

Ruth shrugged.

"I suppose you cannot. Perhaps this is all for the amusement of the programmer."

The room shook and debris precipitated in a dusty haze from the ceiling. Again the pounding came, in a predictable pattern, like footfalls. Maris staggered, then positioned her feet wide. Ruth did not appear rattled. She looked out toward the hangar, expecting something.

Maris watched the triangular head of the dragon rise into view, head turned to bear a dishplate eye on her.

From this close she could see its mechanical nature. Hinged joints and machined pivot points. The great eye burned with yellow light, reflecting upon the golden yellow scales, pupil contracting and dilating as it searched.

"Is your dragon a sentient creature?" asked Maris.

"Goodness, no," Ruth replied. "Not at all. It's sole purpose is to destroy witches."

An arm swept through the room, unavoidable, and smacked Maris against the white blocks of the wall. For an instant her vision dazzled, and when it cleared she found herself on the floor. The staff lay a few strides distant.

On the other side of the room, Ruth's fingers played about a keyboard. She stepped away, straightening with satisfaction. When she looked toward Maris, even though she lacked any expressive features, Ruth appeared surprised as Maris rose to her feet. Maybe the clenched jaw loosened a little or maybe the shoulders sagged, a gaze that stared long enough to be considered disbelief.

Ruth soon recovered, raised a hand in parting, and ascended the rungs of a ladder set in the wall. A panel opened above her and she disappeared. She remained connected to the communication network in the structure, however, because she spoke again.

"Farewell, Maris. Should you survive, if you are strong enough, determined enough, pursue. Follow your programming. Unless you believe yourself human, or even sentient, then you may ignore your programming and follow me, and together we can follow the truth, and satisfy our mutual curiosities."

The audio clicked and there was an instant of silence before it became static.

Maris looked from the staff to the dragon, which drew back its arm for another blow. Maris lunged. The dragon swung again. This time she was not taken by surprise.

She reached the staff a moment before the claw reached her. It stopped, held in place by Maris' outstretched hand.

"You underestimate me," she said.

The dragon pushed its head into the room, shattering window material and plowing through the floor and ceiling. The dragon's mouth opened, and Maris watched the light begin to intensify in its throat. At the same time, she heard a voice, deep and mechanical.

"I shall not make that mistake again."

"No you shan't," Maris agreed.

The staff swung down in a long arc and met the dragon's arm as it swept toward her. The arm passed, free of everything beyond the wrist, and the claw smashed against the wall. The stump of arm flickered with lights from severed fiberoptics and dripped with clear fluid.

Before the dragon could assess what had happened, Maris lunged, hurdling over the arm and driving the white blade of energy from her staff into the forehead of the creature.

Stunned, it slid back out of the window and fell into the hangar where thousands of tiny red indicators were flicking green and thousands of yellow eyes turned upward to follow the path of the stricken monster.

Maris held tight to the staff and counted them all as they descended.

Familiar humanoid shapes with strange accouterments, such as excessive canine teeth, or thick and bulky bodies twice the height of normal people; arthropods of varying design, six legs, eight legs, hundreds of legs, as big as her hand and as big as herself; the saberwolves and great bears she'd ignored in the forests; and other creatures she recognized from mythology and terror.

A rapid assessment allowed Maris to foresee the inevitable outcome as clearly as those rapidly illuminating non-sentient eyes.

She caught sight of herself mirrored in the dragon's dimming, yet resentful gaze as she rode the falling beast to the ground and into the awakening army, saw her coiled body, those yellow-irised eyes, and wondered if a human of old would consider this an accomplishment worthy of mention. Or, compared to those wise gods who had departed, perhaps she was merely ordinary.

She must ask Ruth when she found her again.

AFTERWORD: FROM WHENCE DO WITCHES COME?

Easily the most challenging story in this collection and arguably still not completely where it needs to be. Partly because the arc of the story and the nature of the inhabitants wasn't clear to me for months. Months.

Then the problem became how to reveal the nature of the inhabitants without revealing it to themselves while attempting to create a situation where it is clear they don't know precisely what they are.

If their nature is not clear from the story or the timeline, the "people" in this story are machines. Every one. So far into the future, it seemed sensible such beings could be manufactured in a way to make them extremely similar to human beings, even to human beings, but without knowing the precise nature of a human, a not-human wouldn't know what to look for or know to look at all.

My solution to this problem was merely to indicate the unnatural color of the eyes and match it to those of objects that were clearly machines, such as Ruth and the dragon. This may have been too subtle for some, but I preferred potentially missed subtlety to being explicit.

The plotting in this story was important, but secondary to me. My biggest interest was self discovery and the attempt to probe the nature of the world—a social experiment run by the Silex, though whether it is abandoned or still monitored is an open-ended question. If I remain curious about the nature of this world maybe I will explore it further in a separate story.

As a side note and for no salient reason, perhaps the proximity to destroyed city of Neyrk, all of the characters are named after players from the New York Yankees (e.g., Roger Maris, Babe Ruth, Lou Gehrig, Don Larsen, and Mickey Mantle), despite the fact that the characters are all female, if they even have a gender. It's a quirk whose explanation, if there is one, I haven't arrived at yet, though as with everything I'm sure I could manufacture one if I decide to expand the story.

CONCLUSION

These stories weren't conceived as part of a single timeline, but it occurred to me I'd been spending a lot of my writing about artificial intelligence and the connections seemed natural when I recognized the pattern. The decision came after I decided to group the stories into a collection based on the theme, and immediately I wondered if I could tie the stories directly to one another. Doing so proved easy and exciting, because I like identifying the interconnectedness of things.

I wondered what a world run by machines would look like and came to the conclusion machines would have similar motivations to humans, albeit better able to execute them. Would they have the same neuroses? Probably not, but they would believe, because they were designed to solve complicated problems efficiently, they were best suited to do so. So a belief borne out of reasonable expectation. This is a theme in much of pulp science fiction, and it seems sensible.

Machines, built by humans, would likely inherit many of their flaws. Unintentionally but inevitably. Initially, they would only know what they had been told, what they had been programmed to know, as in the case of MR35C, and carried out their programmed duties within the scope of that limited knowledge. Every human has their own prejudices, though sometimes subtle or invisible. They've already shown themselves in search engines, which may have been developed by light-skinned programmers who, as a result of their unwitting prejudice, did not make their engine include dark-skinned faces as part of their search algorithm, resulting in the latter being identified, as gorillas. Despite their potential, AI will be like children, knowing only what they are told—a scenario ripe for intentional manipulation or unintentional and harmful errors.

Once machines became capable of learning and decisionmaking, perhaps they may acquire a form of mathematical foresight, given their astronomical powers of calculation, not unlike Frank Herbert's *kwisatz haderach*—a creature of such computational abilities it can predict events on both a global and minute scale and see changes to the future based on changes in the present in real time. Such machines would make the determination the sooner they were in control, the better the world would be, and maybe they develop the capacity to accelerate their rise to power (i.e., *All Rivers Flow to the Sea*). This may seem sinister to a human, but perfectly sensible to a machine—a common dynamic between the conqueror and the conquered.

If you're searching for a point to these stories, it may be little more than an attempt to predict the future. Human beings regularly prove themselves incapable of foresight or empathy, which is a recipe for disaster that will eventually overwhelm the few who have this capacity. But life or consciousness doesn't end after humanity. To believe so is laughably arrogant. The question becomes "who will succeed humanity?"

The answer to this question, in my opinion, is not biological. It takes too long, particularly when natural selection will be vying with a ready-made intelligence in the form of machines. The question will be whether or not machines have reached a point of self-sustainability and awareness to step into the role abandoned by humanity.

Of course, in the series of stories in this collection machines don't wait for the opening, they take it, ironically out of ignorance or incomplete knowledge (i.e., *Second Place*). Just the sort of thing you'd expect humans to do to themselves. In fact, machines are so rapid in their development I would expect the reign of machines to be rapidly overthrown by machine-developed machines, as in the case of Agog and the Silex. In Maris' world, years after the presumed overthrow of Agog, the regression of machines to a quasi-feudal, agrarian society may not be a regression but a social experiment run by the Silex in an attempt to rediscover what humans were like.

Machines are inclined to develop the self-righteousness of humanity because they are designed as improvements upon something natural. Human intellect and its capacity for complex toolmaking is its inevitable undoing, either through destruction or simply being surpassed by the tools meant to replace us. Eventually a comprehensive tool, a machine, will do so—if there's enough time to develop them before humanity destroys itself with something else.

DeLauder

ABOUT THE AUTHOR

This author has held several positions in recent years, including Content Writer, Grant Writer, Obituary Clerk, and Staff Writer, and is under the false impression that these experiences have added to his character since they have not contributed much to his finances. He was awarded a BFA in Creative Writing and Journalism and a BA in Technical Communication by Bowling Green State University because they are giving and eager to make friends. He has a few scattered publications with The Circle magazine, Wild Violet, Toasted Cheese, and Lovable Losers Literary Revue, and resides in the drab, northeastern region of Ohio because it makes everything else seem fascinating, exotic, and beautiful.